To Bass ♡

Best Wishes

"Audrey"

What Goes Around

by

Artress Cornmesser

ISBN 0-7414-4405-4

Published by:

INFIⓌITY
PUBLISHING.COM

1094 New DeHaven Street, Suite 100
West Conshohocken, PA 19428-2713
Info@buybooksontheweb.com
www.buybooksontheweb.com
Toll-free (877) BUY BOOK
Local Phone (610) 941-9999
Fax (610) 941-9959

Printed in the United States of America

Printed on Recycled Paper

Published December 2007

Dedication

This book, *What Goes Around*, is dedicated to a beautiful, generous, and courageous woman who loves us all unconditionally. Sister extraordinaire, ILENE HINTON WEBB.

Acknowledgements

I would like to acknowledge the support of my husband, Francis E. Cornmesser, who understands when I stare vacantly across the dinner table, I am plotting yet another tale. I am so grateful for his love and patience.

Special thanks to the people who believe in me and pushed me gently toward my goal.

Mr. Manny Sanchez—Thanks for the ink.

Ms. Tanya A. Fisher—Thanks from the heart, niece.

Mr. Kevon Taylor—Thank you for telling the young people about my book, Baby.

Ms. Ilene H. Webb—Thanks for being true and solid. I am so lucky to have you for a sister.

Ms. Alice Winchester—Proof Reader–Thank you for helping me. You are the best.

Ms. Irene Wilson–Encouraged me to go on and on, and then bought so many copies of my book, Unto the 3rd and 4th Generation, for Christmas gifts.

Ms. Marilyn Epps Bullock–My niece and support in Arizona. Thanks from the heart.

Pamela G–A famous blues singer, yet she takes the time to help her people. Thank you, niece.

Mr. Charley Hinton–Thank you for being a reader, a brother and a friend.

Ms. Michele R. Hinton-Niece and techno teacher, to whom I owe it all.

Ms. Sandra Havens- Cover art. I love it.

Many thanks to numerous friends and relatives not mentioned; you know who you are!

Chapter 1

Regina Henshaw didn't even realize she'd been hit until she saw the blood and her ear started ringing.

Her eyes rolled up to meet the mean slits of her young husband's. Through the loud raspy static of her injured ear, and by following the movement of his lips, she managed to make out the reason for the assault.

"...you better have a job in the next two weeks, or you and these crumb snatchers will be watching *us* pound the pavement instead of a bunch of strangers!"

Prior to the blow, Regina had been absorbed in her favorite activity, feeding their two boys and looking out of the only window in their Brooklyn, New York, stoop.

"Stoop" in New York, meant basements, the lowest apartment in the building with one window that was flush with the sidewalk. Only the shoes and a little bit of leg could be seen from the window of a stoop. Regina knew all about it from watching *Laverne and Shirley* on television when she had been a pregnant teen at home in Kansas.

How funny it had been then, trying to guess what the rest of a person must look like by looking at his or her shoes.

Squiggy, Shirley's faithful sidekick, always said only redheads had nerve enough to wear green shoes, and he would run up the steps of the stoop to get a look at the whole person. He was never wrong.

Regina had been feeding the baby his bottle and watching a pair of green shoes walk past the window, when the blow had come. Ordinarily, when Larry started in about her finding a job, she kept an eye on him. When he reached fever pitch and balled up his fist, Regina was prepared to duck.

And sometimes—not always—but most of the time—if she stayed alert, she was able to dodge the punch.

Green shoes didn't walk by often. Regina was lucky if she saw one pair a week. She'd been gazing at a pair and wondering if the wearer had red hair, when Larry had blind-sided her. It was her fault. She should have been paying attention to her husband's complaints, gauging his temperment, watching his hands. Yes, wherever the blood was coming from was her own fault.

Chapter 2

Regina pressed a hand to the side of her face to stop the bleeding. After three or four minutes of firm pressure, she knew the wound would clot and later scab over, leaving a bruise of yellow and purple to slowly dissipate back into her body.

Being hit was the second worst thing about marriage. Her parents had never so much as given her a spanking.

Even when she had been really bad, their discipline had been doled out in the form of punishments according to the misdeed. There had been lots of timeouts and then no friends over, later there had been telephone and television restrictions along with being grounded, but they had never hit her, that part of marriage had taken some getting used to.

The very worst thing about marriage was being apart from her husband all night while he worked the swing shift in a luggage factory. Regina hated that job almost as much as Larry did, but for very different reasons.

After Larry slammed out of the apartment and stomped up the steps to the sidewalk, Regina tucked their boys into bed and started her nightly ritual.

"Repeat after me, boys. Now I lay me down to sleep..." Since Thompson, the baby, was only six months, and didn't know prayer from pablum, she held his hands together, but Dennis was three years old and bright. Not only did he know the prayer from memory, but other things as well.

"Daddy is mad at us again, huh, Mommy?"

"Say your prayers and forget about it, Dennis. I'll take care of Daddy."

After the boys were settled, Regina curled her body around her husband's pillow and started the nightly daydream. She played it in her mind like a movie, complete with dialogue, starting at the time when she had first fallen in love with Larry Henshaw.

"Little girl, what are you doing hiding out here in this wheat field? Don't you know that everybody in Greenberg is looking for you?"

She tilted her head back to meet his green eyes. It had been two years since she'd seen him up close. She was surprised at the changes in him: the firm brown jaws, the generous lips, curly reddish hair poking out from under his hat.

He was taller than her father. Of course, two years ago she had been only twelve. She was almost fourteen now, and her hormones had answered the call of nature very well.

"Larry Henshaw, don't you dare call me a little girl; you're not that much older than me, and my sheep is stuck in this barbed wire fence. I been trying to get her out for hours!"

Larry took a Case knife and clipped away at the sheep's wooly coat until it was free.

"There," he said, "now go on home so the whole town can stop looking for your little butt."

The whole town consisted of fourteen hundred people, acres and acres of wheat and cornfields, and the deepest well in the whole world. This was Greenberg, Kansas. The famous well-brought tourists from all parts of the world, with its motto that said, *Well, Well, Well.*

Regina Hines' family grew corn in Greenberg, while Larry Henshaw's family raised wheat and cattle. The two families, separated by miles of farmland, had never been what you would consider close neighbors, but since Larry had been voted president of the 4-H club, he had taken to riding his horse through the cornfield to check on Regina's prize sheep.

Regina loved him with a grown-up intensity. To see him break through the corn stalks with the wind blowing his

4

puffy hair and his green eyes sparkling almost stopped her heart. She knew that she would love him forever, but she was just too young to do anything about it. And so, she fast forwarded her dream to the good part.

"Mom, Daddy, Larry Henshaw asked me to go to the May Pole Dance with him. Can I go?"

Mrs. Hines put the dish down and dried her hands. "Regina, you are only fourteen years old, too young for boy-girl dating. You know the rules, sixteen and not a minute before that."

"Why didn't he come to us like a young man should?"

Mr. Hines asked. "Then we could have set him straight."

She had gone to the dance with a group of girls from school and paired off with Larry as soon as she saw him. After a few dances around the May Pole, he had pulled her away from the crowd and into the shadows of the football bleachers.

This was a favorite part of Regina's daydream, and so she took her time, hugged the pillow tight and relived every word, every touch of her first time alone with the man she loved.

"How about a kiss, little girl?"

"Larry Henshaw, why do you keep calling me *little girl*? *I'm going on fifteen years old.*" She wrapped her arms around his neck and kissed him as well as she knew how to prove her point.

"Whoa, there, little girl. I'm a man, going on eighteen, and you're playing with fire here."

"I don't care, Larry. I love you so much. I've loved you for so long! I would do anything for you," she said between kisses.

He pushed her away and then held her at arm's length and searched her face in the shadows. "Really? You loved me for a long time? I sure didn't know it. We'll have to do something about that, little girl."

The nasal drawl of her home-room teacher was the only thing that saved her that night. "Regina Hines, what are you doing over there in the dark?"

Larry dropped his arms to his side and answered for her. "We're just talking, Mrs. Preston. That's all, just talking."

"Well then, talk over here in the light with the rest of the group," she said, giving Regina a long, suspicious look. Mrs. Preston knew about Regina's love for Larry. She had snatched a paper out of Regina's English book one day and read all about it. After school, she'd had the nerve to ask the bus driver to wait up a few minutes while she talked to Regina about an important matter.

"You are very young, my dear, and I expect you'll fall in and out of love a hundred times before the real thing comes along. Meanwhile, love yourself and respect your body. Don't let anybody use it. What you feel now for Larry Henshaw is just puppy love."

Regina had taken offense. "Well then, Mrs. Preston, it may be puppy love, but it's real to this puppy. And I'll thank you not to meddle in my private business." With that said, she had flounced out of the empty classroom and gotten onto the bus.

And now, her home-room teacher was still interfering in her private affairs. She had barely heard Larry say "Meet me in the cornfield" before being marched back to the dance by ole nosy Mrs. Preston. Oh, Lordy, how she hated that hag!

Not wanting to think about old Preston anymore, Regina skipped her dream to a happier time.

"What kept you so long, Larry? I been waiting out here in this cornfield for hours."

"Had a load of homework to do, little girl. Been accepted in a pretty good school after I graduate. Can't let nothing mess that up; my folks would kill me."

As hot as she had been, Regina suddenly cooled off, stood up, and smoothed her dress down with both hands.

6

"Larry Henshaw, you mean to tell me that you intend to leave here after all we've been to each other? To leave *me* for some school?"

"Well now, little girl, I have to get an education, and you don't see any big schools in Greenberg do you? Was just plain luck I got into a good school in New York, where my mother has relatives. I may be able to live off campus and cut costs. We'll see."

Regina wrung her hands. "But what about us, Larry? What about *us*?"

"Sit back down!" He slapped the dirt beside him. They had been having sex in the cornfield since the May Pole Dance last May. At first she hadn't known what to do, but she knew that she had a lot of love to give, so she simply did what he told her to do, like now. She sat back down in the dirt beside him and cried, "If you go, what about us?"

Larry was irritated. "Will you get real! We'll each probably fall in love a hundred times before settling down to one person for life. Least I hope so."

Those had been Mrs. Preston's words to a tee. Regina decided then not to tell him about the baby; she didn't want him to think her stupid.

Chapter 3

In June, Regina stood stoically between her father and mother to watch Larry graduate. It felt more like a funeral than a joyous occasion. Her stomach roiled when he walked across the stage to receive The Most Likely To Succeed Award. Later, when she saw him drive away in his father's brand new 1978 Ford with a girl beside him, she had heaved and vomited right there on the school grounds in front of everybody.

The next day, when Regina was cleaning out her locker for the summer, Mrs. Preston cornered her. "Well, Regina, I see you've gone against all counsel and ruined your life."

Regina had had enough. She just couldn't take any more. She whirled and slapped her teacher just as hard as she could, gathered up her things, and left the building. That was the last time she had set foot in a school.

Little Thompson, fussing to have his diaper changed, brought Regina out of her reverie. It was just as well. She didn't want to think about the bad times that followed when she confessed to her parents that she was going to have a baby sometime in December. She didn't want to think about how her father had cried. It was the first time in her life she'd ever seen his tears. And her mother had taken sick to her bed.

But, they had stood by her. "The bell is rung now, Regina; and you can't unring it. We'll just have to make the best of it."

Making the best of it meant marching her over to the Henshaws' farm and demanding that they make Larry marry her. The Henshaws had been outraged and then downright puffed up.

"Why, our son is away at school, getting his education, and that's what she ought to be doing!" They had looked at her then with such scorn that Regina hated to think about it.

"He should a thought about that before he ruined my daughter!" Mr. Hines fought back. "So you folks just tell me where I can find that boy, so he can make this right."

But no amount of threat or coercion could get the Henshaws to tell her parents where Larry was.

In desperation, Regina's mother had turned to her and said, "Regina, you was with that boy for a whole year and never once asked him what school he was going to? What was you thinking of, girl?"

It was such a loaded question that Mrs. Hines wanted to take it back as soon as it passed her lips. Even the Henshaws blushed at the implication. The Hines' family had gotten no information, and eventually they had gone back home to bear their burdens alone.

No, I definitely don't want to dwell on that, she thought, while changing the baby's diaper and shaking him to sleep again.

Back in her bed, she curled around Larry's pillow and searched her mind for something happy to lull herself to sleep.

There hadn't been, she realized, that many happy occasions the first year that Larry was gone. Oh, she had gotten closer to her mother than she had ever been. Cooking with her in the kitchen and talking about woman stuff had been fun.

"Take special care with your hygiene and grooming, Regina. A pregnant teen is a bizarre enough sight without body odor and bad complexion thrown in the mix."

Regina had taken her advice. She knew that she had not been born beautiful, but she was cute. Compared to some girls, she was even pretty, with her long brown hair, snappy brown eyes, and five-foot-three trim figure. Yes, she had been able to hold her own in the looks department until her fifth month, when her breasts and stomach suddenly shot up and out.

"You look like the letter S in reverse," one of her three friends remarked.

Another wasn't so tactful. "You look like somebody shoved a bicycle pump up your behind and pumped you full of air. I don't want to be seen with you anymore."

Regina knew she had lost her last friend when she telephoned Beverly one evening in her sixth month. "Beverly said she's not home," Bev's mother spoke quickly and hung up.

Mrs. Hines had found Regina crying and looking at the dead receiver in her hand. "What are you calling people to gossip and chit-chat for anyway? You *are the gossip;* grow up!"

That had been the end of Regina's social life. To pass the time, she had taken to marking the days off on a big calendar, reading baby care books, and watching television. *Laverne and Shirley* was her favorite show; they always made her laugh.

Chapter 4

Toward the middle of November, Regina recalled, she had gotten hope in her heart. Maybe Larry would come home for Thanksgiving. All schools let out for Thanksgiving, didn't they?

Since she was entering into her ninth month and was just as big as a house, she had taken to wearing the prettiest smocks she could find and paid special attention to her hair and nails, just in case he showed up. She need not have bothered. November went, and December came in with no sign of Larry.

Her father had a lot to say on the subject. "I suspect his folks got in touch with him and gave him a 'heads up,' and it's just as well, Regina. You don't need a sorry sodbuster like that. He don't have nothing, not even a good character. What do you need *him* for? You can get *nothing* by yourself."

Her mother had been more gentle. "You have the baby, Regina. Get your figure back and go back to school. This is the 70s. Boys want a smart girl with education these days. You have to have more than love and a cute body. Those things won't hold up without a good foundation."

In her head, Regina knew that the old folks were probably right. She'd hardly been in a position to disagree anyway. And so, she had nodded and agreed with everything they'd said.

Regina knew they would never understand her love for Larry that quivered in the pit of her stomach like a pool of jelly. It could not be denied. It was not that she didn't love her parents; she loved them like crazy. They had been so wonderful to her. She smiled in the dark, recalling the memories.

"Mama, the calendar is filling up. I've crossed out all the days, right up to December 20th when the doctor said the baby would come out. When is it coming, Mama? I'm tired of being like this!"

Mama had reached around her belly and hugged her awkwardly. "Honey, doctors are pretty smart, but they don't know everything. That baby won't come until the moon changes and the Good Lord gets ready for it."

Regina had put the calendar away and helped her folks trim the Christmas tree. In a burst of energy, she had surprised her mother by cleaning the whole house for the holidays, wrapping the gifts that didn't belong to her, and chopping all the ingredients for the stuffing, even the onions.

Once in a while, she would let herself think about Larry, wondering if he would be home in time to see her have the baby, but her father had advised her against it. "Don't even think about the scoundrel, Regina; you could mark your baby. When you feel your thoughts drifting toward him, turn them around and think of something good instead. You do have the power to change your mind, you know. We all do."

On Christmas Eve night when the ache in her back woke her up, Regina ignored it. What did a pain in her back have to do with anything? The baby was in her stomach. She hadn't bothered her mother about it either, figuring all the work she had done was causing her back muscles to spasm.

The memory of how she had ruined their Christmas dinner still made her cringe.

"Regina? Do you feel all right? Honey, you don't look so good." Her mother felt her clammy forehead.

She had opened her mouth to tell them that it was just a backache and had thrown up all over the dining room table. Then horrified, she had peed her pants.

Rivulets of water ran from under her, soaking her clothes, the chair, and the rug beneath. The ache in her back grew arms, reached around, and grabbed her belly. Regina

12

tried to speak, but she couldn't. Her tongue was like a block of wood in the roof of her mouth.

She'd had to be lifted from her chair convulsing in pain and literally dragged to her father's old pickup.

Regina didn't remember the ride to the hospital. She didn't even want to recall how cold she had been because they hadn't had time to put on her coat.

She did remember the angry face of the doctor when he'd yelled down at her, "Why on earth did you wait so long?"

The baby had come right there in the emergency room, in the middle of everybody's Christmas Day.

Now that was a memory to dwell on. She couldn't have Larry, but she had a little piece of him, right there in her arms, complete with bright green eyes and a head full of brown fuzz.

"His name is Dennis," she told the nurse, "after my favorite comic strip character the Menace."

Chapter 5

"If there is any such thing as a perfect baby, then Dennis is it," Mrs. Hines remarked to the owner of the Seed & Feed Store.

"Yeah, he's a cute little fellow all right," Seed & Feed had said. "Ole Larry Henshaw can't deny that one. Looks like he hawked and spit him out."

"Yes, well, Larry has never laid eyes on this child to confirm or deny him. He walked at ten months and talked at twelve. He'll be fifteen months in a few days and can do most anything." Mrs. Hines bent down to ruffle her grandson's thick kinky curls.

"Is that a fact?" Seed & Feed mused. "Well, he's missing the best part, I say. These kids grow up so fast nowadays; seems like you just blink, and they are all grown up. Guess he thinks studying to be a lawyer in that big fancy school up in New York is more important than spending time with his own flesh and blood. He'll live to regret it one day. You mark my word."

Regina had been looking at the baby ducks and listening halfheartedly to the conversation. At the mention of Larry, her ears perked up. At the mention of school and New York, she joined in. "You wouldn't happen to know the name of Larry's school, would you, sir?"

"Nope, can't say. All I know is it's up there in New York somewhere."

In May, after all danger of frost had passed, Regina was teaching Dennis how to transplant slips of cherry tomatoes when Larry drove right up to the garden's edge in a little red Porsche.

He jumped out of the driver's seat to lean on the hood with his arms folded across his chest. "Hey, there, Regina, what's going on?"

She had been so happy to see him. She felt like Jesus had come. All the angry things that she had practiced to say if she ever saw him again went right out of her head. All she could manage was a dumb sounding, "Hi."

Larry didn't seem to notice. "Working in the garden huh?" he'd asked conversationally. "Who's your little helper there?"

Anger had shot through her head and loosened up her tongue. "He's no helper, Larry Henshaw; that happens to be your son!" She nudged the child with her finger. "Go on over there and tell him who you are, Dennis."

With chubby legs churning, the little boy closed the distance and stuck out his hand exactly the way his grandpa had taught him to do. "Hello, my name is Dennis Henshaw, and I'm these many." He held up two fingers. "But I'll be these many at Christmas time."

Larry watched the child bite his bottom lip and unfold the third finger. Three years old come Christmas. His head felt light.

Regina had the satisfaction of watching Larry go into shock. The blood drained from his face, and his legs gave way, causing him to lean heavily on the hood of the sports car. She had taken the First Aid class and knew the signs. She still remembered the jingle they had taught her to go by, in case of emergencies:

Face pale? Then raise the tail.
Face red? Then raise the head.

For a moment, she thought about telling Larry to sit down and put his feet up, but changed her mind. *Let him faint*, she thought.

Larry had not fainted, but after a long moment, he bent to the child's level and took his outstretched hand. "Hello back. My name is Larry, and I'm really, really surprised to meet you." Then he had jumped into his little sports car. "Meet me in the corn field tonight, Regina," he told her through tight ashy lips before he roared off.

"What took you so long? Seems like I've been waiting out here in this cornfield forever!" Larry whined when Regina had finally slipped through the corn stalks and sat down beside him.

"Homework," she quipped. "Been inducted into motherhood. Had to put the baby to bed and wait until he went to sleep before I could sneak out. Can't shirk my duties; my folks would kill me."

It did her soul good to fling the very words that he had said to her the last time they had met in this very spot, right back at him. Just like last time, he was irritated.

"That's not funny, Regina. And what do you mean pulling a trick on me like you did today?"

She jumped up and glared down at him. "Now, see here, Larry Henshaw, you came into *my* yard. This is where our son lives, and I would thank you not to refer to him as a *trick*. Take it back!"

Larry took it back. "I'm sorry, Regina. It's just that I was so blown away by it all. Looking at him was like looking at my own baby pictures. I had no idea he even existed. What a shock!"

"You mean your folks never told you?" She sat back down.

"Well, come to think about it, Thanksgiving before last, they came up to school for the holiday, and I asked them about you. My mother said it could have been gossip, but she heard some boy had got you in trouble..."

"And knowing how much I love you, Larry, it never occurred to you to check on me? To find out for yourself if I was okay?" She searched his face for a sign of something.

"Come on, Regina; I know how much you enjoy sex. I figured one of these ole Kansas boys had just stuck it to you. My studies are really hard; there's no time to think about much else. I'm only one third of the way through, and it's getting harder all the time."

16

"Then why are you here now, Larry?"

"Oh, haven't you heard? My father passed away," he told her.

"Oh, my God, Larry, that's just awful!" She flung her arms around him. "We didn't know. I'm so sorry!" She kissed him over and over, giving him comfort, taking on his sorrow. When he slipped his hand under her dress, she didn't have the heart to resist. To the contrary, she'd opened up to him like a flower.

Chapter 6

Regina cherished that part of her daydream. Dreams were all she had left, for that was the last time Larry had touched her. *Getting hit doesn't count for touching*, she thought sadly.

In June, Regina didn't get her monthly friend. She had been too afraid to tell her mother. Too frightened to even think about what might be going on in her belly. Anyway, her mother had been so worried about her father who had been coughing nonstop for weeks, Regina didn't want to add to her troubles.

"Regina, the doctor says your dad has a lung sickness caused by dust. We're thinking of moving out to California near the ocean where my sister lives."

Regina recalled she had been gripped with fear. "California? But what about Larry? When would I ever see him if we moved way out there?"

Her mother had not been kind. "When do you ever see him now, Regina? If his father hadn't passed away, you wouldn't have seen him in May! I swear, girl, if it's possible for a person to grow in reverse, that's just what you've done. Gone from being dumb to just plain stupid."

Not wanting to cause her mother any more grief, Regina had taken to throwing up in the cornfield, out of earshot.

One windy morning in July, while retching and holding on to the tall stalks for balance, she'd heard her father cough behind her. Regina didn't know how long he had been there, but she knew that her secret was out.

"How far along are you, girl?"

There was no calculating to do this time, no guesswork to it. "Three months, Daddy," she'd gasped, "three months along."

In between coughs, her father had called Larry names, some she had never heard him utter. "I'll take care of it this time," he swore. "I'll do it my way."

Later that same day, Regina watched him take down the old shotgun, clean the long iron barrel, and polish the wooden stock to a high gloss.

Her mother, when she found out Regina's condition, had been outraged, but surprisingly calm.

"You hear me, but you don't listen, so why should I waste my breath? I *will* say this, Regina. What you need is a chastity belt—an old fashioned chastity belt with a lock on it."

Now that had really hurt. There had been no more cooking together in the kitchen. No more woman-to-woman chats. Regina stayed away from the house as much as she could. Riding around in the pickup with Dennis and her father had been preferable to the long puzzling looks of her mother.

One day they drove over to the Baptist Church where her father met the minister in the parking lot. After a short conversation, Mr. Hines pulled a big roll of money out of his pants pocket and placed it in the man's outstretched hand. From the truck, Regina strained her ears to hear. "what?... don't know...couldn't tell you for sure...just be ready to come quick," they were saying.

The big, for sale, sign went up on Halloween. Almost every day, Regina hoisted herself up into the pickup and rode with her father around the farm with prospective buyers in tow. When they neared the Henshaw house, he always slowed the truck to a crawl, and muttering something ugly sounding under his breath, scanned their neighbors' property for signs of Larry's car. They never saw it.

One evening after supper—Regina remembered it was getting close to Thanksgiving; her mother was making pumpkin pies, and she was giving Dennis his first haircut—

her father came into the house with an intense look on his face.

"Get your coat on, Regina; it's time to go." He'd said it while taking the shotgun down from its rack.

They had ridden over the dirt road to the Henshaw farm without talking, but the minister had beat them there, and was pacing at the edge of the yard when they had driven up.

"Where is he?" her father had asked the minister.

"Don't know. His car is still parked over there, so he's more than likely inside the house."

It had taken three hard knocks to rouse Larry. He'd come to the door yawning and pulling on his sweatshirt. "My mother is not home; she's..."

And then he saw Regina. "What?" he said rudely.

"Come on out here, boy." Mr. Hines held the gun up for emphasis. "It's you we come to see, not your mama. Gonna give you a chance to make things right."

Larry stepped through the door onto the porch. "What things?"

Mr. Hines coughed and pointed the shotgun at Regina's stomach. "Them things! She didn't get like that by herself, the first time or the second time. It takes two!"

Larry clenched his teeth, balled up his fist, and glared at the man.

Mr. Hines stood hip-shot with the gun cocked. "Swing on me, and I'll blow your head clean off."

Larry's hands slowly uncurled, and Mr. Hines motioned the minister forward with the gleaming gun. "All right, preacher, say the words."

"Ah...We are gathered here in the sight of God and in the presence of these wit..."

"Forget that part, man; just say what's important!" Mr. Hines hollered, making everybody jump.

The minister started over. "Larry Henshaw, do you take this woman, Regina Hines, to be your wedded wife?"

Larry stalled. He was thinking of the many lessons he'd been taught while working side by side with his father, planting corn or mucking out the barn: *Always be true to yourself, son. You can lead a horse to water, but you can't make him drink, son.*

Mouth clamped shut, Larry was wishing his father could be with him now, when he heard the shotgun click. "Say I do, or I'll kill you now, right where you stand. Believe me, boy, I have nothing to lose. Doctor says I'm dying anyway."

The minister was waiting patiently. No doubt he'd been paid a lot.

"Okay then, I do," Larry ground out between stiff, bloodless lips.

Accustomed to officiating at more traditional weddings, the preacher smiled at Larry. "That's fine, son; that's just fine. Now you may kiss the bride."

Regina's father put the gun on his shoulder. "You can forget that part too, Preacher; that's the root of all our trouble here. He done kissed my girl one time too many."

It wasn't until Regina saw the pen shaking in Larry's fingers, with her father encouraging him to sign on the dotted line, that she realized she'd had a real shotgun wedding, just like the Clampetts on television.

"Congratulations, son." Mr. Hines slapped Larry on his back with the butt of the gun.

"Just to show you that my heart's in the right place, I've found a nice little apartment in Brooklyn for you kids to live in. Rent's paid up 'til way after the baby is due. Give you all a chance to get a good start."

Larry had come close to swooning then. His face grew chalk white in the dusk of evening, and his knees sort of wobbled. Mr. Hines was kind enough to help him sit down on the swing. "Don't take this so hard, son; there's a up side to this."

Larry rolled his eyes heavenward. "What?"

"Well, we sold the farm, and we're giving you kids all our household furniture, enough to fill your new apartment. The missus and me are going to California for my health. You're all set up for housekeeping; nothing to buy except food."

Then he'd lowered his voice and whispered in Larry's ear. "You better keep 'em fed too. Mistreat my children, and I swear I'll find you and take you out. That ain't no threat, son; it's a solemn promise."

Regina had heard her father, and she knew that he meant every word. She had been careful in their seven months of marriage not to let her folks know of any discomforts they might have, out of fear for Larry's life.

Chapter 7

The first two months in the apartment were actually the last two months of Regina's pregnancy, and aside from being lonely, there had been no real discomforts.

Every two weeks, just like clockwork, the mailman dropped an envelope in their slot from Larry's mother. It always contained two pieces of paper. One was a check, and the other a note that said *food money* for the dates that it was supposed to cover. There was never a greeting, never so much as a "How is my grandson?" Just the check and the dates.

The only times Regina left the apartment occurred when the checks came. She would bundle little Dennis up in his coat and earmuffs and make her way down the street to the Italian market on the corner where she was careful to buy everything she would need for the next two weeks.

The multitude of unfriendly people made her uneasy. Not one soul ever spoke. On their first two trips down the street, Dennis had shouted, "Hello," and waved at everybody. He was used to people in Kansas stopping on the street and making over him. But the people in New York gave him strange looks and rushed right past them as if he'd said something nasty. Without being told, he had stopped speaking to people on his own.

Larry had stayed in the apartment with them for three nights when they first moved in. Regina suspected he stayed because her parents were still in New York, helping her to get settled, and her father still had the shotgun. It was broken down and packed in a leather carrying case, but he had it still.

The day that Regina's folks left for California was a sad day mixed with spurts of happiness. She had been sad to see them go, but happy when the telephone company installed the black rotary phone.

"We're having a phone put in here, Regina," her dad said, "but it's for emergencies. If you kids sit up here and run the bill up, then you'll just have to pay it. I have a deal with the phone company to pay the service fee; that part will come to me and your mother. That's all we'll be paying, you hear? Rent's paid up here for six months after the new baby comes. That ought to give you kids plenty time to get on your feet."

Regina's happiness plummeted when Larry didn't show up at the stoop that night. Of course, she did realize that he still had a room and three meals a day at that fancy school of his. Not that she knew exactly where it was. Somewhere in New York was all she had learned about it.

When she asked him what the name of the school was, it had been like setting a match to a string of fire crackers.

"*What*? *Why*? *Hell*! It's none of your freaking business!"

Regina could take the verbal abuse; it was nothing new to her. But, what had hurt deeply was the way Larry treated Dennis, or the way that he didn't treat Dennis would have been more to the point. She had explained to the child why he should call Larry Daddy now, but that didn't soften Larry's heart. He rarely spoke one word to the boy all day.

Dennis thought he had it all figured out. "He's a mad daddy, huh, Mommy? A big ole mad, mad daddy."

When Larry did spend the night at the apartment, he slept in his sleeping bag on one side of the bed with a pillow caulked between them for good measure. Any attempt at conversation by Regina was squelched quickly with, "*Shut up!*"

But she loved him still, felt lucky to be sleeping under the same roof with him.

Two weeks before the new baby came was not one of Regina's favorite daydreams. But it did have some happy parts, so she let it play through her mind, if nothing else but to lull her to sleep.

It started with a phone call at a quarter to midnight. "Regina Susan, this is Mama."

Happiness clawed at her heart. Mama only called her by her full name when she had forgiven her. One time Regina overheard her mama telling the cronies in her quilting circle that the "S" really stood for *Surprise*, since Regina had come along after their family of two girls and one boy had grown up and gone away from home. But when she told her husband, he had given her such a horrible disbelieving look, she hadn't dared put it on the birth certificate. *Surprise* had become *Susan.*

"Hi, Mommy," she said, reverting to baby talk.

"What are you doing, honey?"

"Sleeping and dreaming, Mama." Then Regina heard the horrified gasp when her mother realized the mistake she'd made.

"Oh, my God, Regina. I'm sorry! I got the time mixed up. It's Brooklyn that's three hours ahead of Palo Alto. When will I get that through my head? Bet I woke Larry, and he has to get up early for school. Gee, honey, I'm really sorry."

"Don't worry about it, Mama. Larry's not here."

"Not there? Where can he be this late, Regina? It's almost midnight there."

"At school, Mama. Larry stays at school a lot. He has to study hard," she said in his defense.

"Well, Regina, that may be true, but what will you do if the baby comes, and there's nobody there to help you? If I'm counting right, you only have one more week."

"I don't know, Mama," Regina admitted. "I just don't know."

Mama had taken over; she'd called the superintendent of the building, had made arrangements for someone to keep little Dennis if need be, had gotten the

25

address and phone number of the hospital, and had told them Regina would be coming in soon.

It felt so good to have Mama in charge again. Regina had gone back to bed and slept like a rock without the aid of her daydreams for the first time since coming to New York.

On the eve of Dennis' birthday, which was also Christmas Eve, Regina cooked a big dinner complete with baked ham, Larry's favorite meat, and gingerbread cookies for little Dennis.

She was taking the last batch of cookies out of the oven when a loud knock came at the door.

"Who's out there?" she asked through the door, exactly the way her father used to do in Kansas.

"Special delivery," came the reply.

Regina opened the door just wide enough to see the edge of a big box. Couldn't be too careful up here in New York. She listened to the news and knew what could happen.

"Special delivery," the man repeated impatiently, and Regina took off the chain. It was a big box from Palo Alto, California. Her folks.

The man stepped inside and put the heavy box on the floor, and then he stood by the open door, waiting and making small talk with Dennis. "Merry Christmas, little fellow. Boy it smells good in here. Just like my mother's kitchen when I was a kid."

Regina thought that he might be waiting for her to offer him a cookie. She rushed into the kitchen and bagged up three big gingerbread men. "There you go," she said to the shocked look on his face. "I hope you like 'em; they're fresh out of the oven."

He was still staring at the "cookie tip" in his open palm, when Regina closed the door and put the chain on.

People in New York are strange, she thought. *What was he waiting for? Milk to go with 'em?*

The box had truly been something to write home about with receiving blankets and clothes for the new baby right on top. Then came birthday presents and Christmas gifts for Dennis: knitted gloves and slippers with "Merry Christmas" on one and "Happy Birthday" on the other.

Toys and books lined the big box. Dennis tore into every package, wrapped for Christmas or not. He didn't care what day it was. Regina didn't either. When she tried on the fuzzy slippers and the matching robe in her favorite color, she sat down and cried.

Dennis misunderstood. "Don't cry, Mommy; this is a happy box. Here, read me my letter." He shoved a greeting card under her nose.

"How do you know it's just for you, Dennis?

"Because it has little kids on it," he said, jumping up and down.

The card had indeed been a birthday card for Dennis, but on the clean un-printed side, her father had penned a note for her. *You tell Larry what I said still goes. Don't make me go cross these United States after his ass.*

Regina read the catchy birthday poem to Dennis and tried to close the card.

"*No!*" he screamed, "you didn't read it all. There's more!"

"That part is for me, Dennis."

"No, no," he hollered, "it's my card, Mommy, not yours. Read it all!"

To keep the peace, Regina looked at the angry message that her father had written and made up something. "It says be a good boy and mind your mother and father."

After dinner, while looking out of the window for green shoes, Regina gave Dennis a bath and read to him out of *A Christmas Carol.*

"Now, read my birthday card again, Mommy, before you turn out the light." Regina read the poem again and started to close the card.

"No, stop! You didn't read the other part; read it all, Mommy!"

Regina wracked her memory trying to call up the lie she'd told before. "It says you are four years old now, and one day you will be as tall as your daddy."

27

"*Noo*!, that's not what it says, Mommy. That's not what you said before. Now read it right!"

Regina was tired; her feet were big as Dennis' play football, and it felt like the baby was playing soccer in her belly. Her temper flared, "Well, if you know what it says, Dennis, why do I have to read it to ya?" She threw the card on his bed, hit the light switch, and waddled out of the room.

Dennis started screaming then, just as loud as his lungs would let him. "Read it. Read it. Read it to me now, Mommy; read it!" He screamed until the people above them started banging on the pipes. "Stop with the noise, you Goddamned heathens. Ain't youse got no respect for the Sweet Baby Jesus?"

Dennis stopped screaming then and crumpled up the card. "Someday I'll be able to read anything in the whole wide world, all by myself," he said to the man who was beating on the pipes. "Someday, you just watch."

Chapter 8

On January fifteenth, decked out in new mittens and muffs, Regina and Dennis started their four-block biweekly walk to the Italian market on the corner. Regina remembered the day was sunny and cold. She had bent down to show Dennis how to sidestep the slippery patches of black ice still clinging to shady spots along the pavement when the pain grabbed her lower back. Straightening up slowly, she changed their direction and headed toward the superintendent's apartment at the other end of the building.

Dennis pulled back. "No, Mommy, that's not the way to the store!"

Reluctant to bend over again, Regina spoke to the top of his head. "Dennis, remember what we talked about might happen when it was time for the baby to come?"

"Yes, but..."

"No buts, Dennis, it's time for you to act like a big boy like you promised."

Still he pulled back on her arm.

"But I want to go to the store first, Mommy. I'll be a big boy later," he said, loud enough to draw stares.

But this time, Regina had experience and remembered clearly the words of the frustrated doctor just before Dennis was born: *Why on earth did you wait so long?*

Turning, she went directly toward the superintendent's apartment, pulling the disgruntled child behind her.

Mrs. Stein opened the door with a big smile. The memory of her could still make Regina glad. Short wiry blond hair stuck out at all angles from her oval face, and she had a funny way of talking. Mrs. Stein offered her chubby hand, and Regina clutched it. "Come on in here, you darlings. I've been expecting you two. Just call me Mama Stein; some call me the neighborhood yenta," she grinned.

Regina didn't know what a *yenta* was, but figured it couldn't be a bad thing.

"I'm Regina Henshaw and this is Dennis we live in the stoop and the baby is coming." She said it all in one breath without a pause.

Mrs. Stein bent to Dennis. "Well, now, isn't this exciting? A new brother or sister. Come let's you and me call a taxi for your mama."

Dennis was looking important while she let him pick up the receiver and dial a few numbers. "Maybe we'll call your parents in California too, let them know what's going on, since everything is already paid for," Mrs. Stein said to Regina.

"Yeah!" Dennis said, enjoying himself. "We'll call Grandpa too."

By the time Regina climbed into the taxi, she felt comfortable leaving Dennis with Mrs. Stein, not that she'd had any other choice.

From her window in the taxi, Regina got a glimpse of the city and wondered where Larry could be out there. Once the baby came, and she got her figure looking good again, things would be different—a heck of a lot different.

The hospital was bigger than downtown Greenberg. Hundreds, maybe thousands of medical workers, raced up and down the shiny wide corridors. Thank goodness her mama had called ahead. She wouldn't have known what to do.

A cheerful brown-skinned lady in blue scrubs helped her up onto a gurney and whisked her through double doors that said "*Birthing Ward.*"

"Okay, little mother, let's get this show on the road!"

Regina hoped she was a nurse; she couldn't see her name tag. In Greenberg, all the nurses wore white uniforms and little hats. That took the guesswork out of it.

Labor was not one of Regina's favorite memories. It still gave her the willies to think back on how she had suffered the remainder of the day, all through the night and the next day, and still no baby. Realizing she'd gone a little *coo-coo*, but not able to stop herself, she had started screaming at the nurses.

"What the hell's the matter? I already had one baby in nothing flat! Why won't this one come out?"

The startled nurse in blue scrubs had rushed to the phone and called the doctor. Regina picked up snatches of her efficient clip. "...overwrought...highly agitated...no, Doctor, still at seven centimeters...inertia? Yes, Doctor, right away."

Doctor couldn't have been far away; in seconds he was at her bedside. "Mrs. Henshaw, it seems you have stopped dilating at seven centimeters, and you need to be at ten to deliver."

"But *why*?" Regina hollered. "This didn't happen before!"

Doctor took her hand. "Every pregnancy is different, Mrs. Henshaw, and we don't know why these things happen, but if you haven't dilated to ten centimeters in two more hours, we will need to take you to surgery."

"But *why*?" Regina hollered again, louder.

"Because your baby is showing signs of fatigue, Mrs. Henshaw. It's being stressed from wanting to come out. If the heartbeat gets too slow, we'll have to operate sooner."

He turned up the volume on a little box connected to her stomach. "You hear that, Mrs. Henshaw?"

Regina nodded.

"Well, that thumping is the baby's heartbeat. We like it to be between 120 and 160 beats a minute at rest; that is between your contractions. When will your husband be here?"

Regina was too tired to lie. "Maybe never," she panted. "He's at his school."

"What school is that, Mrs. Henshaw? We need to get in touch with him, *now*."

31

"Law school is all I know," she admitted, "law school in New York."

They had actually tried to find Larry. After a long search, Regina overheard someone say, "Well, it beats the hell out of me. I can't find any Larry Henshaw registered in any school in New York!"

Then another voice whispered, "I don't believe she has a husband; just want us to *think* she's married."

Regina had to giggle, just thinking back on it. What they said had made her so mad that she had started to dilate, and the baby came rushing out on a tide of pink water in thirty minutes.

A mewling little boy with her dark eyes and kinky hair. She named him Thompson, which was also her mama's maiden name, in the hope that Mama would realize how much she surely did appreciate all that she had done for her.

Chapter 9

Returning home from the big hospital, Regina was armed with information about birth control. She'd had no idea that there were so many ways to keep from having a baby. In all their talks over cornbread batter and stuffing turkeys, her mama had never hinted at a way to keep from it.

"Just keep your drawers up, and your dress down, Regina, was all she ever said.

Of course, the final and most hurtful advice had come too late. "What you need is a chastity belt, Regina, a chastity belt with a lock on it." That remark, above all others, had cut Regina to the quick.

After the boys were fed and put to bed, Regina poured over the pamphlets. She had six weeks to decide which form of birth control would best suit her and her husband. The doctor had been firm. "No sex before your six week checkup, young lady. Then we'll start you on whatever program you and your husband decide upon."

Regina threw the information titled "Rhythm Method" in the trash. No way was she going to worry about *safe* days and *unsafe* days, and taking her temperature was out. She had never learned to read those little lines on a thermometer. And what was she supposed to do if Larry showed up on her *unsafe* days?

The information marked "Diaphragm" with its funny drawings of female parts and equipment, held her spellbound only because there was no medication to actually swallow. But when she got to the instructions about filling the little rubber cup with jelly and placing it correctly inside her body, Regina was horrified. Why, she could no more do that than she could take out her own tonsils.

The birth control "pill" had a little better sound to it. How hard could it be to take one itty bitty pill every night? Regina had made up her mind that would be the way to go until she read the fine print. Contraindications they called the warnings took up half a page. Most of the big words went right over her head, but she did understand *mood swings, headaches,* and *blood clots* enough to scare the bejesus right out of her.

The new information, and last pamphlet, seemed too simple. One word, "Norplant," was all it said and in smaller letters, "Ask your doctor about this new amazing form of birth control."

Well, she would. And if that didn't work, she'd try 'em all—except that chastity belt—before she let herself get pregnant again.

Six weeks later, Regina still hadn't actually made up her mind until she went to the clinic and sat down next to a young girl with an armful of school books.

"You on birth control?" Regina asked shyly while waiting for the nurse to call her name.

"Oh, yes!" the girl said, smiling. "Sex is good for you, and I'm prone to fat. I need the exercise."

"Exercise?" Regina didn't get it. The girl looked to be no more than sixteen years old.

"Yes," she said, patting her slim thighs. "You know, exercise to burn calories. You can burn up to fifty-one fat calories just by French kissing."

"What do you use?" Regina asked, feeling old next to the girl.

"Norplant," the young girl said. "They just put something in your arm, under the skin that lets out little bits of birth control every day. It's the only way to go. I can't be bothered with that other mess. I have to go to school."

"Norplant," Regina told the doctor when he asked her for a decision.

"Very good choice," the doctor said, and Regina felt knowledgeable and sophisticated.

Mama had cried over the phone when she'd told her what the baby's name was. Right away she had sent a nice camera with the film already in it along with a wad of money. When Thompson was old enough to go out, Mrs. Stein came to the stoop.

"You bundle him up nice and cozy, Regina, and I'll show you and Dennis how to take the train down to the camera shop. You get your pictures; you get some fresh air and nice sunshine. You need to get out more, Regina. A prison this is not!"

That very same evening Larry had come. Both boys had been fed and were sleeping soundly when the impatient knock came on the door. Thanks to Mrs. Stein, Regina was still dressed and looking good. Hair and makeup were in place, and she felt confident and in control.

With one hand on her skinny hip, she flung the door open and demanded an explanation. "Larry Henshaw, where in the world have you been? I had a lot of trouble having the baby, and they couldn't even find you. Said you didn't go to school nowhere in New York!"

For a long time, Larry just stood in the doorway staring at her, the lid of his right eye ticking. Regina stood her ground, waiting for an answer while looking him over. The sight of him made her knees weak. Brown curls falling on his perfect forehead, green eyes blazing and wearing a button-down collar under a camel overcoat, he looked exactly like Harry Belafonte, only taller and better. Just to see him set her heart to galloping in her chest like a herd of horses.

With his eyes still on her face, he stepped through the door and shoved her with both hands. Her feet literally left the floor, and she flew across the room, landing on the little Naugahyde couch that her father had brought from their living room in Kansas.

Larry closed the distance in three strides and stood looking down at her with his legs spread apart and his hands balled up. "You're just a regular baby-making machine, ain't ya? Your whole goal in life is to crank out babies and prevent me from getting my education, ain't it?"

Regina felt her newfound confidence ooze out on one word. "*No*," she whimpered, spraddle-legged up from the little couch.

"Answer me, I can't hear you!" he screamed down at her.

"*No*," she said louder, completely deflated.

"Well, then," he said nastily, "that's good to know. I could have sworn you was trying to ruin my life." He reached in his coat pocket and pulled out a folded sheet of newspaper.

"This is called classified ads. You look through this and find a job, any job. I don't give a damn what kind."

Regina recalled he had stayed with them three days on that occasion. Anyone who didn't know better would have thought they were a loving, happy, young family.

One morning, Larry had insisted on taking out the trash.

"There's not enough trash in our can to bother going to the dumpster with, Larry," Regina said. "Why don't you wait until it's full?"

But he had gathered up the few pieces of paper and had gone out anyway. Later, Regina found out, he had gone from the trash bin to Mrs. Stein's place and thanked her for helping his family in their time of need.

Mrs. Stein thought that Larry was just building his case so that she would have something good to tell Regina's father when he called from California to check on them. Mrs. Stein didn't care for Larry. She often referred to him as that *schmuck*. Regina didn't know what a schmuck was, but she figured it had to be a bad thing from the expression on Mrs. Stein's face when she said it.

For hours Regina studied the classified ads. "I might not be the sharpest knife in the drawer," Regina said, using one of her father's old sayings, "but I can read English, and this, by God, ain't no English!" She had thrown the newspaper on the floor and got up to feed the baby.

Later Larry had spent a long time interpreting the information in the classified ads for her to understand. "BKLYN stands for Brooklyn, Regina. You can call any number with BKLYN behind it and not pay extra. In other words, it is not a long distance call for you.

"LI means the job is on Long Island; and since you live in Brooklyn, it would be a toll call for you. Unless the job looks mighty good and pays well, try to stay close to Brooklyn. Cuts down on travel time and expense.

"NYC means New York City.

"MHTTN means Manhattan Island.

"QNS stands for Queens. You should be able to find work without going way out there...Just start in the Flatbush area and work your way back this way, Regina."

"But, Larry, won't I have to pay for calling Flatbush? It's not Brooklyn."

Larry got so flustered that he rapped her on the knuckles with a butter knife. "Don't you know nothing, girl? Flatbush is part of Brooklyn, just the name for a neighborhood is all, like Bedford Stuyvesant is. How could you be here all this time and not know that?"

But he might as well have been talking about Russia, and her fingers ached where he'd hit her with the knife. Regina's temper had flared, "If you hit me again, I'm going to tell my daddy."

Larry jumped up. "Oh, you're going to tell your daddy on me, huh? Well, let me give you something to tell the bastard." He stood up, full height, balled up his fist and swung. The blow caught Regina just below her right shoulder blade. He hit her so hard, the whole right arm went numb. Regina had to look, to assure herself that it was still connected to her body.

"There now, you can tell him that I hit you for being stupid. It's your own fault for being dumber than dirt!"

Regina didn't learn much about the layout of New York, and she didn't tell her father for fear of Larry's life. But she did learn a few things about her husband and how to protect herself from getting hit. Just listening to what he had to say wasn't enough. She had to pay attention to the tone when his lips got tight and then watch both hands closely. When they balled into fists, she had to duck quickly.

Chapter 10

Regina hugged the pillow to her chest and smiled proudly in the dark. She had gotten pretty good at dodging most of Larry's blows as long as she stayed alert. There were a few exceptions, like the time Dennis had made him so mad, he'd struck without warning.

Thompson was three months old, and Larry had spent a couple of days with them to help Regina look for a job.

"Regina, you only have three more months here before the rent comes due. You have got to get a job. I'm trying to finish undergraduate school, and dammit, it's not easy. My mother cannot afford to pay this rent; she is already buying all your food, without a word of thanks from you, I might add."

Before Regina could think of something to say in her own defense, Dennis had appeared out of the second bedroom and grabbed a hold of Larry's hand. "Come quick, Daddy, and see the baby; he knows how to smile now!"

Larry had let himself be led to the baby's crib where he stood staring down at the grimacing drooling infant. "Oh, hell," he'd said, "that ain't no *smile*. He's probably full of gas bubbles, just like his mother."

Dennis didn't know what *gas bubbles* meant, but he'd been so hurt by the tone of Larry's voice that he'd forgotten his manners. Pulling his little hand out of Larry's big one, he stepped back and screamed at his father, "He is too smiling! I don't care what you say, 'cause you're just a mean ole daddy, and I hate you!"

Larry had turned on his heels, stalked out of the children's room right up to Regina, and hit her in the eye.

"You better teach that little hoodlum some manners, Regina. He's got a smart mouth on him."

A week later, after the eye had gone from red to purple to yellowish-brown, Regina was on her way to the Italian store with the children and a pair of dark glasses on, when Mrs. Stein stepped into her path.

"Hello, Regina. Not feeling too good are you?"

"Feeling fine, Mrs. Stein. How about yourself?"

Mrs. Stein ignored the question. "Then why the dark glasses, Regina? Are you sleepy?"

Regina took the shades off. "No, Mrs. Stein, I hurt my eye, and the glasses cuts down on the glare."

Mrs. Stein didn't buy it. "Regina, do you know what *battered woman* means?"

"Not really," Regina answered, adjusting the baby on her hip. "Why?"

"Because I think you might be one, Regina. He hit you, didn't he?"

Regina didn't answer the question, but that didn't stop Mrs. Stein. "I have poor eyesight, but I am not blind, so I can see he hits you a lot. No?"

"Yes," Regina admitted, "sometimes."

Mrs. Stein smiled. "Then I was right, so you are in luck."

Dennis was getting impatient. "Come on, Mommy, let's go to the store!" Regina pulled back on his hand. "Wait a minute, Dennis," she ordered the child.

Then she turned to Mrs. Stein and asked, "What do you mean, *I'm in luck*?"

"You go on to the store, dearie. I'll tell you all about it when you get back."

After the children were in bed, Mrs. Stein had come to the stoop. Regina remembered she still had the happy look on her face. "My dear, let me tell you why you are a poor, lucky girl." Mrs. Stein said, "A few years ago, someone with a lot of money put up a beautiful apartment complex in Bedford Stuyvesant, not too far from here. It's a lovely place with real grass, gated, and all fenced in for children. There is a childcare service right on the place for working mothers to leave their children. They even help you find a job if you qualify to live there. But to qualify, you must be a battered woman. And you are a battered woman, little *schicksa*, if ever I saw one."

She took Regina's hand. "All you have to do is show them your eye, and all that other stuff on your arms, and presto, you're in like Flynn!" She smiled, pleased to be of help.

The smile was erased when Regina asked, "But what about Larry? Can he come too?"

"Larry who? The *schmuck*? My dear, that would be like locking the fox in the hen house." Then in a kinder, softer, gentler voice, she asked, "What do you need him for, honey? He beats you, and Dennis don't like him either. I know I'm a meddling old yenta, but when you was in the hospital, Dennis told me that Larry was a mean ole daddy. He didn't make that up, Regina; children tell the truth about how they feel. You should listen to your child."

"But we're *married*, Mrs. Stein. Larry is my husband, and I love him to death! Anyway, it's my own fault if I get hit. I need to learn to duck faster, not make him mad by talking dumb, find a job and pay our rent, and keep the kids quiet when he is home. Larry studies *hard* at school to be a lawyer. Can't you understand that?"

The old lady shook a crooked finger at Regina's nose. "Regina Henshaw, don't you ever say that through your teeth again. No woman deserves to be hit; nothing is your fault! God gave you a beautiful body. You gave that *schmuck* two perfect children out of it. That should be enough right there to make him lick your feet and worship your body, not beat on it! Nobody has a right to do that, honey."

"Well, I'm getting pretty good at ducking," Regina replied, missing the point entirely.

Mrs. Stein took a deep breath to calm herself. Young people were a piece of work. "You should think about those beautiful apartments, Regina. Every woman whose husband ever so much as said *boo* to her, is trying to get in there. You don't have to be married to apply either, just abused."

The baby let out a squeal, and Regina stood up. "Thank you for telling me, Mrs. Stein. I have to see about the baby now."

"Let him fuss a minute, Regina. A little crying is good for his lungs. I want to tell you a story."

Regina kept standing; she didn't like her baby to cry. "It won't take long," Mrs. Stein insisted. "I tell you, and then I go."

Regina sat back down on the edge of her chair. Mrs. Stein started her story.

"Once there was a single mother with two children, living in these apartments, just like you. She was a beautiful girl, nice and clean, always paid the rent on time. Had her place fixed up real nice too. She took good care of her children, and then she lost her job in the shoe factory.

"The girl came to me, in tears. But I just manage these apartments. I don't own them, so I couldn't help her. The poor girl only had enough money set aside to carry her for two months. After the first month passed and she still had not found another job, she got desperate and paid a man to beat her up so that she could get into the complex for battered women."

The baby had stopped crying, and Regina gave Mrs. Stein her undivided attention. "What happened?"

"Well," Mrs. Stein went on, "I'm sure she told the fool just to hit her enough so that she would qualify—you know a black eye, a couple of bruises on the cheekbone? That's all he had to do—all she paid him to do. But the man must have been a real abuser. Once he started beating on the girl, he didn't stop. Messed up her eyes, broke both cheekbones, knocked out teeth. She had a bruised liver and damage to other organs inside her poor body. One arm, I forget which one, had a *green stick* fracture, the very worst kind. You see, when an arm is just plain broken, the bone can be set back in place, and the doctors can put a cast on it.

But with a *green stick*, the arm is mangled with torn muscles and ligaments. *A holy mess!* The bastard even broke her leg!"

Regina gasped at the gory descriptions of the girl's injuries. "Did she die?"

"No, but I took the bus to the hospital to see her; and I tell you, Regina, she didn't look a thing like herself. Any fool could see it was going to be years before she worked again."

Regina was looking at Mrs. Stein with horror. She had never heard anything so awful in all her life. "Why didn't the girl have him put in jail and sue him, Mrs. Stein?"

"She did press charges, and they did put him in jail for a short time, but at the hearing, the man said that he kept beating her because she never did tell him to stop. 'That was the deal,' he said to the judge. 'She paid me to hit her until she said stop.'

"Now, I ask you, Regina, could you say *stop* with both of your jawbones broken?"

Regina felt her face. "No, I don't believe I could," she admitted.

"Exactly!" Mrs. Stein exclaimed. "And that bastard knew it too. I think he enjoyed beating that girl to within an inch of death's door. Other people thought so too, but the judge said we had to stick to the facts. The public defender laughed so hard the judge called a recess. That same afternoon, the case got thrown out for, 'No grounds to sue.' And the son-of-a-bitch walked. I'd like to give him some ground, Regina, six feet of it."

The memory of that story always made Regina feel uneasy, although she didn't know why. She moved on to less disturbing memories, complete with animation.

It was lunchtime, and they'd been having a birthday party for Thompson. Regina taught Dennis the words to the birthday song with one eye on the clock. When the second hand clicked to twelve forty-seven, she lit a little blue candle, forced it down into a warm sugar cookie, and they started singing.

"Happy birthday to you...Happy birthday to you...Happy birthday to Thompson, Happy birthday to you." Then, just for fun, Regina started the second verse.

"How old are you...How old are you...How old are you, Thompson, How old are you?"

Dennis started laughing and tickling the baby's cheeks. "Say five months, Thompson, watch my lips and say f-i-v-e."

They had been having so much fun, watching the drooling baby and eating sugar cookies. It was a balmy May day, and Regina remembered she had left the door open, hoping to catch a spring breeze, when Larry slammed into the apartment and spoiled their fun.

"Regina? You didn't go to *work?*" His bellow could be heard all over the building. "I got the job all set up for you in that shoe factory right here in Goddamn Brooklyn! Why in hell didn't you go?"

There it was, the dreaded shoe factory. The same people who fired that beautiful girl and caused her so much grief. Regina got spunk in her spine just thinking about that poor girl and all her injuries. She screamed across the room, a safe distance from her husband.

"*No*, I didn't go to work in that place because I couldn't find anybody to keep our boys. Mrs. Stein said her eyesight wasn't even good enough to watch for diaper rash, and she already has a job as manager of these places. I'm telling you, Larry Henshaw, Mrs. Stein is crazy about the kids, but she don't want another job!"

"*So what?*" Larry hollered. "The paper is full of people looking for babysitting jobs. Get one of 'em!"

"But, Larry, I don't want to leave our babies with somebody we don't even know." Regina was crying frustrated tears. "I just can't do it, and I won't do it!"

Dennis noticed Larry was sneaking up on his mother by degrees. While they yelled at each other, Dennis had been wise enough to roll the baby stroller into the kids' room out of harm's way and stick the pacifier into Thompson's mouth.

Then he lay down on the floor to listen intently at the open door.

"Then that settles it," Dennis heard his father say, "I'll have to quit school and get a job to pay this rent, you sorry little life-wrecker you."

The sound that followed left no doubt in Dennis' mind that his mommy's head had been knocked wide open. He curled up like a baby and started sucking on his thumb, something he had not done in two years.

The next time they saw Larry, he was carrying more stuff than Regina knew he owned: ski poles and skis, shoes of all description, roller skates, ice skates, a basketball, and more books than Regina had ever laid her eyes on except in the Greenberg Library. He dumped everything in a corner of the little bedroom where it reached clear up to the ceiling.

In a sad soft voice, he said to Regina, "Well, you got your wish, life-wrecker. I had to drop out of school and take a job in a luggage factory working on the swing shift. I hope you are happy now."

Regina could barely hide her glee when she lied, "Oh, that's too bad, Larry. I'm so sorry!"

The next month was the happiest time in Regina's married life. She spent hours thinking up hairstyles that might catch Larry's attention. Food money was wasted on perfumed bath gels when good ole Ivory soap would have done the job.

Mrs. Stein gave her a *Good Housekeeping* magazine with a basic hamburger recipe in the cooking section. Regina discovered that five pounds of hamburger, carefully mixed and rolled into balls or shaped into loaves and patties, could save her enough money on groceries to buy a couple of miniskirts. She got so good at manipulating the budget; the clothes cost more than the food. If she kept working at it, Regina felt sure, with the help of God and Estee Lauder, her husband would eventually come around, notice her, need her, and love her.

One Saturday, on Larry's night off, Regina went to the corner where he sat reading the biggest book she'd ever seen. Looking good and smelling good, she felt empowered, sure of herself. "Honey," she said in her most enticing voice, "It's late; don't you think we should go to bed?"

Larry finished reading the page before he turned and sneezed full in her face. Before she could wipe the spittle out of her eyes, he sneezed again, spraying her hair and new blouse with tiny drops of moisture. He dropped the book and grappled in his pocket for a handkerchief. Finding none, he looked back at Regina. In that instant his chest caved in and a string of sneezes gushed out of him so fast, it was hard to tell where one explosion stopped and the other one started. Larry was gasping for oxygen when he finally managed to catch enough breath to talk in spurts.

"What...ever...that shit is...you're wearing, Regina... get rid of it...before it kills me."

So, the fragrance and bath gel had gone into the garbage can, but she doubled up on the makeup for good measure. Nobody, except Marilyn Monroe maybe, ever wore more pancake and eye shadow.

One day Dennis looked in Regina's face and asked, "Mommy, where are we going?"

"Nowhere, Dennis. Why?" she asked.

"'Cause you're all dressed up like a clown," Dennis said.

After that day, Regina cut back on the blue eye shadow, but not the pancake, because she didn't think there was anything cute about freckles on a black girl. Larry didn't seem to notice, one way or another. He spent the days sleeping and reading thick books in his corner, and the nights working in the luggage factory. On the rare occasion when he did share her bed, he always slept in his sleeping bag with a pillow stuffed between them.

It's all for nothing, she thought while rubbing the little lump of birth control in her upper arm and staring at the back of Larry's curly head. *He is never going to love me again.*

The very next morning, while Larry was eating hamburger and eggs, Regina told him, "Larry, I'm thinking of moving into the battered women complex. They have childcare right there on the place, and they would help me find work too. Mrs. Stein is sure I could qualify. She said she would put in a good word for me. Then you could go on back to your school and do whatever it is you're so mad about."

Larry looked at her for a long time. Then he threw his fork so hard it went into the wall, up to the hilt. Regina watched the handle vibrate and hum a kind of musical tune. Suddenly, he was standing over her. "And what do you think Mrs. Stein's good word for you will do to me?"

Regina shook her head. She hadn't thought it would involve him at all. Mrs. Stein said husbands couldn't go there. Confused, she looked at him and shook her head again.

Larry started slowly. "Let me tell you one thing, Regina. After Mrs. Stein puts her good word in, which means she will tell them that she is a living witness to my being a wife beater, you'll be flitting around in your fancy new apartment, while I rot in jail for spouse abuse."

He was picking up speed. "And that is what you want, Regina, is it not? To ruin my life completely is your goal. It wasn't enough for you to trap me with one baby. *Nooo*, you had to have *twooo*! And all you had to do was tell your father that you didn't *want* him to force me to marry you. All in this world you had to do was *refuse*! *Refuse*, Regina, instead of standing there saying *I do* like the airhead that you *are*!" He was going full throttle now, dead heat.

"So, why not go to the battered woman's complex? Have me arrested and thrown in jail? Get me a big criminal record so that no respectable law school in the world will let me in, huh? Go ahead and finish me off! It's your method of operation, your damn M.O."

"No, Larry, I wouldn't let them put you in jail," she cried. "I wouldn't press charges against you. Nobody could make me do a thing like that."

Larry stared at Regina for a long moment. "This might be a little hard for you to grasp, but you wouldn't need to press charges. It would be a matter for the State, completely out of your hands."

Regina was confused again; she couldn't figure out why right seemed to be wrong. "But all I want is for us to be a family, Larry, for us to love each other and the kids. That's all I ever wanted in my whole life. Is that so wrong?"

"No, Regina, there's nothing wrong with that, but you need to do whatever it takes to bring these things about."

"What, Larry, what?"

"First you need to stay away from that old vulture of a woman, Mrs. Stein. Don't take any more of her advice and don't listen to nothing else she has to say. Can't you see she's jealous of you? She's *old*, almost blind, and dried up like a prune. You're young, fresh, and pretty with a knockout figure. Anyone would be jealous of you. Can't you realize that?"

Regina had been thrilled to know that Larry thought of her as beautiful with a knockout figure. Thank God, all her efforts to make him notice her had not been in vain. She would promise him anything, and she did.

"That's good, Regina. That's good. Now in return, I promise not to hit you unless you make me. But you have got to find a babysitter and a job. Is that clear?"

She trained her eyes on his handsome face; nothing could compare to the love that welled up in her heart. "Yes, that's clear."

Larry trained his eyes on her blue eye shadow. What a *cluck*! In all his dating life, she was the dumbest black girl he had ever spent time with. What was blue eye makeup supposed to do for dark brown eyes? And that red stuff on her cheeks? He had never known a black girl to blush. If she did, how could you tell? It was all so pathetic somehow.

"Oh, and, honey, you should give some thought to going back to school, night school maybe. New York has more schools than any other city in the nation. You need to find one and get in it."

"Yes, Larry," she lied. He was always calling her dumb. Well, sometimes he could be dumb too. If she worked in the daytime and went to some ole school at night, when would she get to see her children?

But Regina kept such thoughts to herself. This was the longest conversation they'd ever had in seven and a half months of matrimony, and she had said more than she'd ever said before without getting hit.

Progress is definitely being made, Regina thought, punching at the pillow.

What she had to do now was figure out how to smooth things over from making him so mad yesterday. It had been two weeks since their long conversation about the battered woman's shelter, and he'd only hit her once in all that time. Actually, to be fair, you could say that the *window frame had hit her*, since it was the sharp edge of the wood that cut into her cheek when he'd slapped her—all because she had been looking at those green shoes, Chuka boots actually. She had been so excited to see a pair of green *boots* walk past the window; that was a rare sight! If she could have gone up the steps like Squiggy and seen the whole person, she was sure she would be wearing a dark green trench coat, with a green felt tam to match, pulled down around a head full of red hair.

It was her own fault; she should have been paying attention to her husband. "I'll make it up to him," she mumbled to the pillow just before sleep claimed her. "I'll cook him some ham and potatoes tomorrow."

The next day, her children had just finished lunch, and Regina was cleaning up the dishes when Larry bounced through the door with a big smile on his face. It was such a foreign expression, Regina looked around for some place to duck.

"Good morning, everybody!" he chirped, and Dennis, sensing something was wrong, started to his room.

"Good morning, yourself," Regina said, warily. "You look happy."

"Oh, I am, I sure am." Larry smiled while watching Dennis walk the other way.

"Guess you had a good night at work then, huh?" Regina asked, cautiously.

"Oh, yes, great night. I figured out the answer to all our problems. I got you a job."

She started to ask what kind of job and what about the children, when he raised his arm and hollered, "Give me a chance to finish before you start whining!" Giving Regina a glimpse of the old familiar Larry and realizing he had slipped out of character, he cleared his throat and started over.

"Now, honey, there is a girl working in *piecework*— that's the sewing area—who is leaving. I asked the foreman if they had replaced her yet, and he said no. So I told him about you and how bad you needed a job. He was grateful. Fact is, you're already hired. They're not even going to interview you because they know me, see?"

Because she didn't see, Regina was afraid to answer.

"Well, don't you see?" he badgered, "all you have to do is show up and start sewing, and whamo, at the end of the week you get a paycheck. The pay is pretty good too." Larry stood in front of her, grinning. "Well, can you get any better than that, Regina? You got a job and a paycheck coming without even leaving the house."

She found her voice then, "But, Larry, I don't know how to sew. I never sat still long enough to learn."

The masquerade fell away, and he screamed, "Goddamn it, Thompson could do it!"

Regina ducked out of pure habit and watched while he checked himself, regaining composure. "Look, there's a whole wall of machines, Regina. They don't look anything like your mother's Singer. There is a big long needle, a pedal, and a spool of thread bigger than a box of Morton's salt. For God's sake, all you have to do is sit there, press the pedal with your foot, and sew a pocket into two feet of satin material. Then you toss that into a basket; that's it, your piece is done. Someone else down the line will sew another piece and connect it to your pocket—so on and so forth until the suitcase lining or backpack lining, or whatever the hell you're working on, is complete. Even a child can do it."

Regina nodded and washed the cereal bowls over and over, waiting for him to tell her the part about childcare. Surely the factory must have a place for the children to be kept if they expected her and Larry to work all night on the same shift.

Thinking on it, she thought it just might be the answer to their problems. They could all ride to work together like a real family, and she would check on the children every two hours at break time instead of drinking coffee. Yes, she just might try piecework; it could be just the thing to bring her family close together.

"Is that nod a yes?" Larry pressed her.

Regina gave him another slow nod and a whispered, "Yes."

"Good, you have ten days before you start to work. Whew, that is a load off my mind! I really appreciate this, Regina."

Larry yawned and started toward the bedroom. Regina didn't want to, but he was forcing her to broach the subject. "Larry?"

"Later, Regina, I'm whipped."

"I just need to know how close the childcare area is to where I'll be working." He stopped still, one foot raised in mid stride. She spoke timidly to his back, "I will need to check on the boys about every two hours. I figured if it's not too far, I could do it at my break time."

He spun around so fast; both arms flew out from his sides. "Regina, are you daft? It's a factory! There are things in there that could kill grown men, much less a child! Danger signs are posted all over. They wouldn't let a child within a mile of that place!"

Rage made her throw caution to the wind. She took the risk of getting hit. "What do you expect me to do then, Larry? Leave the kids here alone all night? Well, I won't do it, and you can't make me!"

The smirk on his handsome face was misconstrued as a grin. Regina relaxed when he said, "I have a plan, Babe, I really do. After I get a few hours sleep, you come on in the bedroom and wake me up. We'll talk about it."

He had better have a darn good plan, Regina was thinking as she went about the morning tasks of caring for her children. She knew a thing or two of her own, thanks to Mrs. Stein, who had waited until Larry left the stoop with his basketball one day and knocked on her door.

"Hello, Regina, it's a beautiful day, and I'm going to get out for a while. Will you and the boys come with me?"

Regina had hesitated, thinking of the warnings that Larry had given her about her only friend. "Well, I don't know, Mrs. Stein; I really need to cook."

"Oh, we'll be back in plenty of time, dear. Come and treat your babies to some nice sunshine vitamins; they stay indoors much too much."

"My children get their vitamins every morning," Regina bristled. "I never miss a day."

Mrs. Stein threw her wiry head back and laughed. "I can believe that, dear. You're like a mama lion when it comes to your children, but there is a certain kind of vitamin D that comes only from the sun. You can't get it in a bottle. Babies need it to develop good bones."

They had a wonderful outing, soaked up lots of sunshine, and somehow ended up in Bedford Stuyvesant near the battered women complex. Mrs. Stein was excited. "We're so close, dear. Let's go in and have a look around. I've always wanted to see inside."

Regina balked. "Larry told me to stay away from this place; he could go to jail."

"Oh, what does Larry know?" Mrs. Stein snapped. "These people are not in the business of putting husbands in jail! Anyway, we don't have to give them our names."

Regina was persuaded; they walked around the block, and there before her eyes were more flowers than she had ever seen in one place. The grass had to be real for a man to be cutting it with a lawnmower, didn't it? They walked up the ramp to the entrance. Stunning apartments flanked both sides. One bedrooms for single women, two and three bedrooms for women with children, and a laundry area, larger than her whole apartment. But it was the play area that took her breath away. Someone had hauled in sand to make a real beach in one corner. There was room to ride small bikes or maybe skate. Little padded swings hung from the ceiling for the ones not yet walking. A huge playhouse, with real furniture, stood in one corner under a false palm tree. Regina had actually gone inside and sat down.

They had toys Regina hadn't even known existed—tricycles made like fire engines and cars. Dennis crawled into a red one and went speeding around the curvy little road, grinning and honking his horn.

The whole room was closed in with glass, or something that looked like glass, making it possible to play outside in any kind of weather.

When a little brown boy asked Dennis, "Wanna play?" Dennis had looked at her with wide questioning eyes, not knowing what to say.

"Say, yes, Dennis," she'd told him, while realizing, for the first time, that her son had never played with children his own age. "It's okay."

Back in the office, Mrs. Stein had asked for some literature to take to a friend. They had given her all sorts of papers and pamphlets with phone numbers and hints about how women could protect themselves. "Tell your friend to call or come here anytime, day or night; we'll be here to help her. That's what we're all about."

After that day, Regina felt empowered, so Larry's plan had better be a good one because now she had a choice.

Chapter 11

After lunch, followed by story time, Regina put the boys down for mid-day naps and then she tiptoed into the bedroom.

Larry was not asleep. When she got close enough, he reached for her hand and pulled her to him. "Come on, lay down here; let's talk," he'd said softly.

This new Larry took some getting used to. It had been a long time, over a year maybe, since he had touched her lovingly, and the sleeping bag was nowhere in sight. Her heart started to gallop, and she looked around for the big pillow that always kept them separated. It was under his head.

"Come on down here now." His voice was tender, but at the same time the grip on her hand strengthened, and he jerked straight down on her arm so violently that something went "thunk" in her shoulder.

The pain made her eyes water. When one knee buckled and slammed into the iron railing of the bed frame, Regina fell across his chest, but managed to keep her head up and her neck stiff. She was trying to tell him that he was hurting her, but he had wound a hank of her long brown hair around his fist and was using it to force her face down on to his. Teeth cut into both her lips, and she tasted a memory.

"Regina Susan Hines," her mother said, "haven't I told you not to run through the tall corn stalks? The sharp leaves can hurt you? Now you've gone and cut your lip, and it's bleeding like sixty! Stop licking the blood and don't swallow any; humans aren't suppose to eat blood. That's what animals do!"

When Regina came up out of the reverie, Larry was using his body on her like a battering ram. The dainty blouse had been torn right up the middle, and the loose material was used to keep her arms pinned down. Between thrusts, he bit hard on her breast and pinched the tender flesh on her stomach with his thumb and forefinger.

Pure instinct told Regina that there was something wrong with the act, but maybe he had wanted her for so long, he'd just gone a little crazy. Once she had heard her mother say, "They should make little hats to fit a man's fly because all his brains are in his pants."

And so she held on, through the pain and turmoil and a mouth filled with blood until he'd spent himself with a groan and rolled away.

After three attempts and a boost with her good arm, Regina managed to sit up and place both feet gingerly on the floor. In agony, she'd put one foot ahead of the other until she was standing over the toilet, spitting blood and flushing before stepping under the shower in what was left of her clothes.

Larry started talking in a soft gentle voice while Regina was dressing herself in a soft flowered mu-mu. "Why so pensive, Regina? You haven't said a word since we made love. I mean, you *did* want to make love didn't you?"

Regina dipped her chin, yes.

"Good, good. Then let the record show that Regina girl wanted to make *love*, and today she finally got what she wanted," Larry said, playing at being a lawyer. "Now, that's cleared up, let us move on to the next problem—babysitting.

"Regina, I want you to call your folks today; now would be a perfect time and ask them to keep the boys for a while. Tell them that you have a job working on my shift, and that we need help for three months until we get on our feet."

Flabbergasted, she tried to make sense of what he'd said. "But when? How? Thompson is only six months old! Larry, you must be joking!"

"I have never been more serious, Regina. You'll never trust anyone except your mother to keep the boys, and we both know it. I figure you could take the train, have a nice long trip seeing states that you've never seen before. It will be a good experience for Dennis too."

He reached for the phone and held it up to her. "Now, make the call."

Regina took the telephone with trembling fingers and dialed. When her mother answered on the first ring, she panicked. She hadn't had time to get a story together and didn't know what to say off the top of her head. All she could manage was "Hi, Mom" three times.

After the third "Hi, Mom" Mrs. Hines, sensing something amiss, yelled, "Regina Susan, what's the matter with you? Are you sick?"

"Yes, I mean no, Mom. I'll feel better in a couple of days. It's nothing to worry about. I called to tell you that I have a job on the..."

Mrs. Hines cut her off. "A job? But Thompson is only six months old, and Dennis is..."

"Mom, I know all this. What I'm trying to say is I really need you and Dad to keep the boys for a while until we get on our feet. No more than three months, Mom. Three months, tops."

"Well, I don't know, Regina. I'd have to ask your dad and your Aunt Cynthia since we're living on Social Security here in her house."

"Let me speak to Daddy, Mom; put him on." While she waited for her father to come to the phone, Regina covered the mouthpiece with her hand and told Larry, "I have to ask my dad. What do I tell him?"

"Tell him the train from New York will be rolling into San Francisco in three days, and you and the boys will be on it. Ask him to meet you there. You have to be back here and on the job in ten days, so time is of the essence."

Mr. Hines was not happy to get the news. "So, he's making you go to work to pay the rent, and that baby ain't even six months old yet. He's a pitiful excuse for a man, Regina."

"It will only be for three months, Daddy, and I'll send money for food and formula. Will you help us?"

"Well, I won't turn my back on my own flesh and blood, so you bring 'em on. We'll make out somehow."

At dinner, Dennis watched his mother out of sharp green eyes. "What's the matter with your leg, Mommy? You got a owiee?"

"Yes, Dennis. Eat your food and don't worry about it. It will be okay in a couple of days."

"Why don't you just put a Band-Aid on it, Mommy? So it can get all better?"

Regina searched her young son's face. For a second she was tempted to tell him that she would put a Band-Aid on it, if she could find one big enough to crawl into. "Stop talking and eat your food, Dennis," was all she felt safe enough to say.

When Regina told Dennis that they were going to see Grandpa, Dennis ran to his room and threw all his toys into a paper shopping bag. "I'm ready," he said, dragging the bag into the living room behind him. "Let's go!"

"Whoa there, little man," Larry said to his son without looking at him. "You'll have to wait until tomorrow when I can get the tickets. Hope your mother can pack as fast as you can."

After Larry left the apartment, Regina sneaked over to Mrs. Stein's place to let the children say good-bye.

"You are some lucky little devils," she said, kissing Dennis on the forehead. "I always wanted to go to California, but I don't think I'll ever make it out of New York now. I'm too old to cut the mustard anymore."

"I'll be leaving the boys with my folks, but I'll be back in five or six days," Regina assured Mrs. Stein. "Don't worry about our rent. I know it's due in a couple of weeks, and I'll be able to pay it because Larry got me a job in the luggage factory on the same shift as him."

Mrs. Stein looked her over, "Oh, I don't worry about you, little chickee; you're a good girl, but why can't Larry pay the rent with his paycheck?"

Regina bristled. "He has to buy our train tickets, Mrs. Stein, and he needs to get back in school. Larry is going to be a big famous lawyer someday."

Mrs. Stein kissed her cheek. "Oh, lawyer-smawyer, tell me what else is new? Take good care of yourself, Regina; your children need you."

The train station was a scary place. Regina hadn't seen so many people in one place since her folks had taken her to the fair in Kansas.

"Stand right here in this spot and don't move," Larry told Regina. These Red Caps work for tips. I can check your luggage myself."

Regina hitched the fat baby up in her arms and bent down to Dennis, "Take a hold of my dress, Dennis," she admonished, "and don't let go for nothing! If you got lost in this crowd, you would be a old man by the time I found you."

When Larry returned, he had two tickets, one for Regina and one for Dennis.

"Babies get to ride free," he said, "because they don't need a whole seat."

"Larry, are you telling me that I have to ride for more than two days with Thompson in my arms? Well, I can't do it! Don't they have a place for people to sleep on this train?"

She was drawing stares. "Keep your voice down, Regina, and don't be such a hick!" Larry whispered. "The train has a sleeping car, but we can't afford no crap like that; it costs a fortune! Anyway, the seats recline just like a bed, and you can lay Thompson on one-half of Dennis'. His butt ain't big enough to take up a whole seat."

Regina started to put the tickets in a side pocket of the diaper bag that she shared with Thompson for a purse. Then she suddenly stopped.

"Larry, my ticket says one way *only*!"

At the same time a voice called, "*All aboard*!"

Larry scooped Dennis up and set him just inside the door of the passenger car. "Come on, Regina! You need to get on and find your seats. The train is getting ready to take off."

Rooted to the ground, staring at the train ticket, Regina found it impossible to move her feet. "This ticket says 'one way' Larry. You was suppose to get me a *round trip ticket!*"

He reached for her face with both hands and kissed her lips tenderly. "I know, honey, but I ran short of money. All you have to do is call me when you get to California. Tell me the day that you want to come back, and I'll send you another ticket. Nothing to it."

"Well, okay then, I guess that's all right." Regina clung to his shirt with her free hand, soaking up the kisses. "You know I love you, don't you, Larry?"

"Yes I do," he told her, while helping her up the steps into the train where Dennis stood waiting, "and right back at you."

Larry had been right; the seats were wide and comfortable. With a few extra pillows she'd managed to make a cozy bed close enough to keep a hand on Thompson while Dennis sat by the window.

From her seat, Regina looked out over Dennis' head, hoping to get a last glimpse of Larry. But there was no sign of him in the multitude milling around the platform.

I love you, she thought, remembering his last tender kiss. *And you finally said you love me too. Maybe not the words, but it means the same thing—right back at you. Old lady Preston would call it ditto or vice versa or something.*

She settled back in her seat and mulled it over in her mind and then decided to try it out on Dennis.

"Dennis, let's play a game," she said.

"Okay, Mommy," Dennis beamed.

"Just say I love you."

"Okay, I love you, Mommy," Dennis grinned.

"Right back at you!" Regina said, peek-a-boo style, and clapped her hands.

"What's it mean, Mommy?" Dennis was confused.

"It means I love you too. Now it's my turn. I love you, Dennis."

"Back on you," Dennis said, forgetting the words.

"No, no, Dennis, say *right back at you.*"

But Dennis had reached the end of his attention span. "I don't want to play that game anymore, Mommy, it's silly." And he turned back to the window.

Riding the train with two children turned out to be hot, grueling work. After four or five trips, Dennis thought he could go to the bathroom on his own, and he did, but Regina still had to take Thompson every time she needed to go. The stamp-sized toilet was just big enough for one person to squeeze into. But she solved that problem by setting the baby in the little stainless steel sink and keeping one hand on him.

Scenery didn't hold much interest for her either. Chicago looked exactly like New York to her, Iowa exactly like Kansas. *And if you've seen one cornfield, you've seen 'em all,* she thought, when they rolled across Nebraska.

Dennis loved the farms with horses and sheep, but they only caused pangs of homesickness in Regina.

After three whole days they had reached the mountains, finally something of interest to her. Regina had never seen anything so big, and she wondered how in the world they got there. *Bears and lions must still be living in those hills. I mean who could ever find them back up in there?* And as hot as it was, some mountains still had snow on the tops. She made a mental note to ask her father about it.

After four days of riding on the train without a bath, Regina could smell herself. She felt she was second only to Thompson who could clear the coach when he needed his diaper changed. Self-conscious, she tried to keep her arms down, thinking that if she ever got into a shower, she'd stay all day.

Chapter 12

Regina was getting anxious about the time. Larry said in three days they would be in California, that she could visit with her folks for three days, and still make it back to New York in time to start her job in the luggage factory. But five days had passed, and the train was just pulling into San Francisco. She would have to cut her visit short.

"Be careful, Dennis!" Regina cautioned her son too late as he leaped from the train's top step into the waiting arms of her father. Mr. Hines was only half as big as he had been the last time she'd seen him in Brooklyn. She watched him march away with her ticket stub in one hand and Dennis on his shoulder to claim their bags before turning to greet her mother.

"Hi, Mom," she said as she kissed her cheek. "How is Dad doing? Looks like he lost a lot of weight."

"Oh, he has," Mrs. Hines said, reaching for Thompson, "but he's holding his own. We have excellent medical care, thanks be to God and your Aunt Cynthia here."

Regina turned to the brown-skinned woman standing beside her mother and stuck out her hand. "So you're Aunt Cynthia. Well, I'm pleased to meet you. You look just like my mother, only taller," *and more beautiful*, Regina thought, taking in the crisp white linen pant suit and perfect haircut at a glance.

Aunt Cynthia ignored the hand and took Regina in her arms, hugging her so tight, Regina could feel the gold bracelets dig into her back. "Welcome to California, my dear. I'm so very happy you came."

She exuded such love and smelled so good, Regina burst into uncontrolled tears. Horrified at herself, she pulled back.

"Oh, gosh! I'm sorry, Aunt Cynthia." She brushed at a wet spot on the linen lapel. "I need a shower so bad. I'm afraid I'll get you dirty."

"Nonsense," Aunt Cynthia said, and she pulled Regina to her and hugged her again. "Never dwell on things beyond your control, child. We'll take you home and get you as good as new. In a couple of hours this fussing will be all for naught."

Riding along in Aunt Cynthia's pink Lincoln Continental, Regina got a glimpse of the city.

"Why are all the houses linked together?" she asked no one in particular.

Mr. Hines answered. "Not a lot of space here, honey. San Francisco is sitting on a hilly peninsula; they have to build high and tight."

"It would sure be nice if you could stay long enough to visit Chinatown," Cynthia said. "It's a city within itself, Regina. Five minutes in Chinatown is like taking a trip to the Orient."

With her mind on Larry and the new job, Regina couldn't work up too much enthusiasm for a bunch of Chinese people, but the Golden Gate Bridge got her full attention. "My gosh," she gasped, "I thought it would be painted gold, but it's a dark red. How long is it, Daddy?"

"Little over four thousand feet, and they have to paint it with special stuff to repel the rust. Takes a group of men a whole year to paint it from beginning to end. Thing is, because of the wind and salty water, the bridge has to be painted once a year, and so the men just start all over again; the painting never stops. It's a regular career for some. Little Dennis here could go to school for bridge painting, make a good living, and never be out of a job."

Mrs. Hines pointed toward the bay. "See that island out there, Regina? Well, that's a jail. They took the whole island and made a federal prison out of it. Alcatraz they call it, and it's full of all manner of thugs."

"Take a good look at Alcatraz, Regina," Cynthia said; "it will soon be part of San Francisco's history. I hear there are plans to close it down."

"Then what will happen to all the thugs?" Regina wanted to know.

"Oh, they'll be absorbed into the hundreds of prisons around the United States is my guess."

After two hours, Regina knew more about San Francisco than she had ever learned about Brooklyn, New York, in eight months. She thought it might be fun to take Dennis for a ride on a trolley car or a boat ride on that beautiful blue ocean, but for now the traffic on 280 South was so terrifying she closed her eyes and thought about Larry. She counted the three hours time difference off on her fingers and wondered where he might be. Eight p.m. in California, and the sun was still blazing in the west, but she knew that it was eleven and pitch black in Brooklyn. Regina decided she didn't care what time it was, she was going to call Larry just as soon as she could get her hands on a telephone.

"Look, Mommy, horses!" Dennis yelled.

Regina opened her eyes just in time to see the street sign "Sand Hill Road" before the big car turned right and started up a winding road. It was better than a picture postcard; trees of all description grew everywhere. Houses bigger than most motels that Regina had ever seen nestled among them. Dennis was right—horses, even goats grazed here and there. Once she thought she spied a sheep.

"What are those trees with black-looking leaves, Aunt Cynthia? I've never seen one of those before," Regina asked, in amazement.

"Japanese plum trees, Regina, but there's no fruit on them. They are just for show."

The house turned out to be a mansion set into a hillside overlooking Stanford University. Aunt Cynthia had given the first floor to the Hines and kept the second and third floors for herself. Regina thought there must be enough room for her whole 4-H club in the downstairs area alone.

"Wow, Aunt Cynthia, you must be rich," Regina said, looking around the spacious living room for a telephone.

"I wouldn't say *rich*, Regina, but I chose education and real estate over love and poverty. Looking at your beautiful children, I wonder if I made a mistake, but it's too late for that now. I made my choice, and I'm willing to live with that."

"And thank God she did," Mrs. Hines said, coming into the room. "I don't know what we would do without Cynthia. Come take your bath, Regina, before the water gets cold."

After baths and a light dinner, Dennis insisted on two bedtime stories, and then he wanted to talk. "I love California, Mommy. Grandpa said I could ride a horse."

"I'm sure you will, Dennis; now go to sleep. It's getting late." *And later in New York*, she thought, calculating the time again.

Finally, Regina thought, as Dennis' eyelids fluttered to a standstill. She rushed out of the room, poked her head into the nursery just to be sure Thompson was sleeping, and came face to face with her mother, rocking the sleeping child in a brand new cradle.

"Mom, you don't have to rock Thompson to sleep; he goes very well all by himself. And why did you buy him a new bed? He'll only be here three months, tops. You should have saved your money."

"Well, Regina, we can always sell it. What I want to tell you is how sorry I am for going over the edge when I found out you was pregnant with this lovely child. He is a bundle of pure joy, looks so much like our people. I can't imagine the world without him in it. I hope you will someday find it in your heart to forgive me."

"Oh, don't worry about it, Mama; it's all in the past. The night you called me and said, 'Hello Regina *Susan,'* I knew that I was forgiven."

"Is that so, honey?"

"Yes, the only time you call me Susan is when I'm back in your good graces."

"Well, I never paid that no attention; guess you know me better than I know myself."

"Yeah, Mama, goodnight, and thanks for everything." Regina tiptoed quietly down the hall to her room. Damn what time it was in New York, she was calling Larry anyway.

The telephone receiver shook slightly in her hands; she was exhausted. She hadn't had any real sleep in a week. After telling Larry to send the return train ticket, she was going to crawl between Aunt Cynthia's pretty sheets.

Carefully, Regina dialed the long number direct, straight through. She would worry about the phone bill later; she would pay her folks back with part of her first paycheck from the luggage factory.

Of course, there was a good chance Larry wouldn't be home, and she would have to call again. But at least she could tell him that she had tried.

After five rings, fearing her suspicions were right, Regina lowered the receiver. Halfway between her ear and the cradle, she heard a loud, "*Lo!*"

Bringing the receiver back to her ear, Regina spoke quickly, "Larry, is that you?"

"Whooo?" came the heavy accented question of a sleepy sounding man.

This wasn't Larry. Somehow she had dialed the wrong number. "I'm sorry, sir, I must have the wrong num..." He hung up before she could finish. *Can't much blame him,* Regina said to herself, *it must be after two o'clock in New York.*

She looked around the strange room for something to write on and found a big yellow legal pad inside the little double doors of a credenza. After saying each number out loud, Regina wrote them down in big inch-high figures and then working slowly, she marked them off as she dialed.

This time there would be no mistake. It was answered on the first ring.

"What!" a man said rudely. For a split second, Regina was too shocked to speak. A lecture from her mother flicked across her mind. "Regina, people can't see that you don't feel good over the phone. It's in here for our convenience. Better not to answer at all than to pick it up and talk nasty. That's rude!"

A loud, "Who the hell is this?" restored her speech. She knew she had the right number, but could this be her house?

"This is Regina Henshaw. Is this 1677 Lucern Street?"

"Yeah, ain't you the same bimbo that called a few minutes ago?"

Regina got mad. Bimbo was not a very nice word; she knew that much. "Yes, I called. I thought I had the wrong number. I wanna know what you're doing sleeping in my house and answering my telephone like that. Is Larry Henshaw there? Put him on!"

It was the man's turn to be mad. "What do you mean *your* house? My family, we live here almost one week now; the phone people they come later today to give us our new number, and I don't know no Larry..."

He paused, thinking. "Wait a minute, wait just a Goddamn minute," he said and then laid the phone down. Regina could hear him talking to someone.

"Honey, do we know anybody named Larry something?"

A sleepy voice answered, "Yes, the nice man who let us have this apartment and sold us all this furniture, Mr. Henshaw. I think his first name is Larry. Who wants to know?"

Regina heard the words of the stranger sleeping in her bed, probably on the sheets that her folks had sent her for Christmas, and part of her started to die. By the time the rude man came back on the line, her heart was beating way below normal.

"Now look," the man was saying, "there used to be a Larry who lived here, but he had to move quick 'cause his family all die. I pay two hundred dollars for all furniture, and I got my receipt, so don't try no funny stuff with me."

"Do you know where Larry Henshaw moved to?" Regina asked in a thin high voice.

"I donno," the man answered, "all's I know is he don't live *here* no more!" With a bang, he broke the connection before Regina could say another word.

She had heard him hang up, knew he was gone from the line, yet she gripped the receiver, kept it pressed hard against her ear hoping for a miracle. If she kept the line open, he might pick up the phone and say "Sorry, lady, I made a mistake." She had to hang on to the line!

California sunshine was blazing through the trees.

Mrs. Hines had the boys out walking the winding road, looking for horses. Aunt Cynthia had been at work for hours, and the house was quiet except for the persistent hacking cough of Mr. Hines, reading his paper in the kitchen. It was almost noon.

Regina is sure sleeping a long time, he thought. *Think I'll just go check on her; she really needs to eat something. Last night she didn't eat enough to keep a bird alive.*

Coughing his way down the hall, Mr. Hines knocked lightly on the door of Regina's bedroom. "Honey, are you awake yet? It's almost noon."

When she didn't answer, he pushed the door open a crack and peeked in. "Oh, sorry, Regina, I didn't know you was on the phone."

He started to turn away from the door and then stopped. Something wasn't right. That bed hadn't been slept in, and she still had on the same clothes.

Mr. Hines stepped into the room, "Regina, honey, why didn't you go to bed? Who is it you're talking to?"

Then drawing nearer, he saw that her eyes were vacant, unblinking. The hand that gripped the telephone receiver to her ear was ashy and bloodless.

He clapped his hands in her face. "Regina! Regina Susan! Give me the phone!" There was no response, no indication that she had heard a word.

Mr. Hines was frantic, coughing and sobbing out loud. With one hand under her knees and the other around her frail shoulders, he lifted Regina onto the big bed where she stayed stiff, still in the sitting position with a death grip on the receiver, stretching the short cord to its limit.

"Oh, my God," Mr. Hines cried. "Oh, Sweet Jesus! My girl done gone round the bend!" and he went running and coughing to find his wife.

Chapter 13

From the narrow telephone booth, Larry watched the train crawl slowly away from the crowded station. He didn't want to call his mother too soon; the damn thing might have a flat. Well, maybe not a flat, but anything could happen to it the way his luck had been running lately. He waited until he saw the last car clear the station before he dropped his money in.

Mrs. Henshaw answered on the first ring, "Ha'lo?"

"Mom, it's Lawrence."

"Yes, son?"

"It's done, Mom. Everything went as planned."

"Are you sure, Lawrence?"

"Yes, Mama, the end of the train just cleared the station."

"Good, son, how did she take it?"

"Same as usual, she's dumb as a mud fence in a rain storm. Even the kid has more smarts."

"All right now, Lawrence, you listen to me; from this day on, keep yourself protected. Better yet, just leave the girls with round heels alone."

"*Round heels*, Mom?"

"Yes, son, the ones that roll over like a Goodyear tire as soon as you touch them. They're loose, stupid, and don't know what it is to work toward a goal in life. Their sole purpose is to get their rocks off and trap a good–looking man such as yourself in the process.

"Please, son, read your letter again. Read it over and over until it sinks into your brain, and then you get up and get back in school to fulfill your real father's dream. Don't let his death be in vain. I live to see you fulfill his dreams to be a lawyer, and I refuse to die and leave this world until you have accomplished that. Your step dad, Mr. Henshaw, was of the same mind. He wanted this for you; he loved you as if you was his very own son.

"There is money from him set aside for you, but you can't get it until you get twenty-six years old."

Larry was surprised and irritated at the same time. "Twenty-six, Mom? Why? I need money now. You know I'm working in a luggage factory to make ends meet, had to drop out of my classes and all kind of crap. If there is money in my stepfather's will for me, then hell, I need it now!"

Mrs. Henshaw was laughing on the other end before Larry finished his tirade.

"Well, son, I was just thinking about the conversation me and your stepdad had, before we set that trust fund up. He said to me, 'Hope, when that boy sees the age restriction on this thing, he's gonna have a fit.'"

Larry let out a grunt in the telephone booth. His mother ignored it. "Now, son, it's all in writing; your stepdad and me sort of made a pact; if I out lived him, then I would guide you to complete our goal and vice versa. Now, Lawrence, you know what to do, but just so I won't worry about you, tell me the first step."

"Well, Mom, I'm going to take out the letter, read it twice, and then go about my father's business."

"Good, son." She sounded tearful. "I plan to rent out the farm soon so that you will have enough money to finish school. We'll talk about that later. For now, just clean out your little love nest and get yourself down to business."

"Will do, Mom, bye." Larry stepped away from the telephone booth and looked around. Another train, headed for another destination, was boarding passengers where he'd last seen Regina. "Good damn riddance," he muttered under his breath and headed for the parking lot.

Hope Henshaw broke the connection with her finger and said a prayer out loud. "Thank you, God; he's going to be something if I have to die trying." She put the receiver in the cradle and sat staring at the phone, thinking back on her life and how far she had come.

Hope's earliest memory was of herself at five years old, standing on an apple crate washing dishes in a sink that was big enough for her to take a bath in, while her foster mother sat nearby, drinking something from a fruit jar, overseeing the job.

"You better wash that pot over, Hope; it still looks greasy. You need to learn to do things right the first time around. Life ain't gonna be easy for you because of the way you started out, so work for perfection in everything you do. Maybe then you'll have a chance."

Hope rested her little arms on the rim of the big sink and looked at her foster mother. "What you mean, started out? Started out *how*?"

For the first time she heard the story, but not the last time. The details had been thrown in her face every time she made a mistake, until she got old enough to be on her own.

"Well, your mother, whoever she was, wrapped you up in a sheet and left you in a big enamel dishpan on the Armstead's porch. The Armsteads were the only Negroes around here with real education and any money to speak of. Times was hard then, still is. I suppose your mother thought the Armsteads would want a little girl since they only had one child, a cute little boy about the age you are now. But the Armsteads were both schoolteachers, working from sunup to sundown, and they didn't want any more children, even if it was a girl. Some said they didn't keep you for fear you might have had bad blood, but I don't know how true that is.

"Anyway, they took you, dishpan and all, to the welfare office, and their little boy had a fit. He had been the one to find you on their porch, and he felt like you belonged to him. They say that kid cried and held onto you in that pan until his father spanked him, and they took you away. Guess he never forgot 'cause it's going on six years now, and he still comes over here every Sunday with enough candy to rot your teeth right out of your head."

Hope understood then why her friend Lawrence Armstead came to the foster home to play every Sunday. He never played with the other children, only her; and he always brought something good like Tootsie Rolls or Baby Ruth, her favorite.

"I named you Hope," her foster mother said, enjoying herself, "'cause you was such a scrawny little thing, I thought you might need it." She laughed and slapped the table. "But if you don't learn to wash dishes any better than you're doing 'em today, there ain't gonna be no *Hope* for you."

Their love had sort of sneaked up on them. Hope couldn't remember when hers started. Maybe it had always been there, a buffer between them and the rest of the world.

"When you get eighteen, I'm taking you away from here," Lawrence said to Hope, kissing her face and her fluffy hair. "You're mine. I found you, and I'm going to keep you safe."

One Sunday afternoon he pressed her, "Are you thinking on it, Hope? We only have a few weeks left before your eighteenth birthday, and you still haven't said 'yes.' I already paid the justice of the peace in Haskell, Oklahoma, to marry us. Last week I rented a nice trailer for us on the outskirts of Haskell. I'll be able to come home from school two or three times a week to be with you, care for you like I always have. When I get my degree and pass the bar, I'll be the best Negro lawyer in Oklahoma, or the whole world maybe."

They were married on her eighteenth birthday against his parents' wishes.

"Screw 'em," Lawrence said, when Hope held back. "They got married when they wanted to, and we're gonna do the same."

Life in the trailer was so wonderful that Hope didn't think heaven could be any better. She was a good cook and kept a sparkling clean house, thanks to her training in the foster home. Lawrence came home three times a week and took care of her, just as he had always done since he'd found her in a dishpan on his porch.

When Hope was absolutely sure, she told him that they were going to have a baby. Lawrence had been so happy that he'd cried and kissed her stomach. And then he'd gone across the street to introduce himself to an old spinster lady by the name of Dora Henshaw, and he asked her to look out for his wife on the days that he couldn't make it home from school.

After that, Hope and Miss Henshaw always waved at each other when they were both outside working in their tiny yards. One day the old lady asked Hope about the baby.

"He's due the end of June," Hope told her. "Least I'm praying it's a *he*."

"Well, don't you worry about a thing, dear; whatever you have will be perfectly suited to you and that lovely husband of yours. God don't make no mistakes, and he don't make no junk. So, you just put your mind at ease. But just in case you *might* have an emergency, I have a phone over here that you are welcome to use at any time. But I don't expect you'll need it, dear; you look like the perfect picture of health. Your skin has the first blush of the ripe peach. There is nothing more beautiful than a lassie reproducing life."

Hope thanked Ms. Henshaw, not only because she was a good motherly neighbor, but also because Hope felt safe, comfortable, and loved in her perfect little world of unbelievable contentment and happiness.

And then, without warning, the storm came.

Larry took his sweet time going back to the stoop. He felt like the world had been lifted from his shoulders. What he really wanted to do was celebrate, go to a bar, and get stinking drunk.

He might just do that, too, after he read his letter again. Larry had promised his mama that he would go straight and read the letter. Get his priorities back on track. And he'd never broken a promise to his mother.

Back in the stoop, Larry headed for his duffel bag and the waterproof pocket where he always kept the letter: instructions for his life.

The apartment was peaceful, no Dennis staring at him with wide, knowing eyes; no Regina, whining and smelling like dead roses, no dirty diapers stinking up the place.

Larry unfolded the pages carefully to keep the creases from tearing. One day soon, he would have it laminated. Kicking off his shoes, he stretched out on the bed and started reading in the middle of the page.

The first part, *My dear son, I waited until you was old enough to understand before writing you this letter, etc.,* had been committed to memory long ago. He read slowly letting the words sink into his heart, renewing his purpose in life.

I was six months pregnant with you, sitting on the steps of our little trailer waiting for your father to come home from school. It was a beautiful day, not a cloud in the sky—when Ms. Henshaw waved at me from across the road. I smiled and waved back, but she kept on waving. I couldn't figure out why she kept waving at me like that so I started walking toward her, and then I heard what she was saying. She told me to go back and get into the bathtub because there was a tornado coming.

Well, at first I couldn't believe my ears; it was a sunny day, no sign of a storm, but lucky for you and me, I was used to taking orders, being raised in a foster home and all.

I whirled around and headed back to our trailer. Before I reached our steps, the sky turned black. We didn't have a bathtub, so I crouched down in the little shower and covered up my head. And then it hit me. If there is a tornado coming, where is Lawrence? Is he in front of it or in back of it?

I crawled out of the shower and turned on our little radio, an RCA Victor that Lawrence had since his childhood. It didn't look like much, but sometimes, when it was foggy, that little radio could draw stations all the way from WWVA in Virginia, and KDKA in Pittsburg, Pennsylvania. I plugged it in the tiny bathroom and jumped back in the shower.

But all I got was static. Now I tell you that to tell you this. If you are ever in a tornado, son, do *not* rely on the radio for information because the electricity from the storm blocks out all the radio signals, and all you hear is static. The thing to do is watch the animals. Horses, cows, sheep—even dogs and chickens will be running in the opposite direction. And that is how I knew your father was in front of the tornado. For sure they were both headed in the same direction. I could only hope and pray that he had got a late start from school and was behind it.

The sky got darker, almost like night, and there was noise like two freight trains coming. Our little trailer started to lose things. I heard part of the roof go, and then I could hear the steps that your father had made and bolted to the frame rip loose and rattle down the road. I tried to get up from the shower floor and peek out of the little bathroom window again, but something held me down. Later I learned it was pressure from the tornado, the same pressure that kills all the animals.

It was quick, no more than two or three minutes. When it was quiet and I could stand again, I made my way to the front of our trailer and flung the little door open. Everything was flat. Not one house was left standing on the other side of our road. Where Ms. Henshaw's house used to be, there was nothing; even the foundation was gone.

Every kind of animal lay dead with their feet up from the pressure of the tornado. There was a bulldozer up on our road where men had been doing construction work. When they came back to the job, that bulldozer was buried deep into the ground. A big heavy thing like that. The trees didn't have a chance. Not a one was left standing.

The tornado had cut down one side of our road, took out everything and everybody, while our side of the road remained almost untouched. Ms. Henshaw was found a half a mile away, still in her bathtub, in the middle of somebody's living room. She was dead.

It was a few hours before the Red Cross got around to check on us. I gave them a description of your father, what he was wearing, and the make and model of our car. They helped me down into the yard and told me to look under the trailer, and there was your father, dead.

The coroner pieced the story together. He told me Lawrence had been in front of the tornado. He had made it home to us and managed to get out of the car just seconds before it was twisted up and flung halfway across town. The force of the wind ripped his clothes off, still he kept coming. He had made it all the way across the road to where our steps used to be, when the tornado tore Ms. Henshaw's place asunder. It took silverware from her kitchen and drove soup spoons all the way into telephone poles. Knives and forks were buried into trees up to the hilt. They found one of Ms. Henshaw's dinner forks buried deep in your father's chest, the tines resting in the left side of his sweet heart. If the steps had been there, he could of made it.

People told me not to cry so hard, that it was God's will and to be thankful that Lawrence didn't suffer. I mean, how long can you last with a dinner fork in your heart? Be grateful death came quick. They didn't know that not only was I crying for Lawrence, I was crying for me and you too, son.

There was one big mass funeral held in the town where over a fourth of the people had died. Mr. Henshaw came to bury his sister and to settle what was left of her estate. I invited him over to share the last pot of coffee I had in this world.

He asked me about my plans for the future. I had to admit I had two weeks of food left in the trailer and enough money to carry me another three or four weeks. After that was gone, I didn't know what I'd do. One thing I knew for sure, I meant to keep my baby safe. I made a vow to raise you to follow in your father's footsteps so that his death would not have been in vain.

Mr. Henshaw told me about his farm in Kansas. Told me that his wife had been dead a long time, and I was welcome to come live with him. And I did. A few weeks before you was born, we went over into Pratt, Kansas, and got married.

When you got here, Mr. Henshaw gave you his name; it was just easier if everybody in the house had the same last name, but on your birth certificate, legally, your name is Lawrence Armstead, Junior. When you finish high school, we expect you to take your real father's name and go on to do great things. Let nothing or nobody stop you from reaching your goal. We will help you all that we can to be the best Negro lawyer in the world. Anybody who tries to stop you is your enemy; remember that, son.

I want you to keep this letter some place safe. When you have doubts, take it out and read it again. Don't talk about your plans to other children. This is family business. Your job is to go forward and finish your father's dream, Lawrence. Look neither to the right or the left, but straight ahead.

Your Loving Mother
Hope Armstead Henshaw.

The letter almost hypnotized him. The need to achieve stole over his heart like a religious experience. He put the letter away and picked up the phone.

"Mrs. Perez? Larry Henshaw here. Do you still want to rent the apartment? Okay then, tell your husband you can move in tonight. Yes, tonight. There is two weeks paid up; you can have it. I am asking two hundred cash for the furniture and all the other stuff. The telephone can stay, but you need to have the number changed as soon as possible."

The Dean of Men at Columbia Law School pumped his hand, "Good to have you back, Lawrence. Does this mean your personal problems are solved, and you're ready to get down to business?"

"Yes, I guess you could say that, John," Lawrence said, feeling important because he was one of a few men on campus on a first-name basis with the great man.

"Good, good, Columbia would hate to lose you, Lawrence. I suspect you'll be our bright shining star someday. You show a lot of promise."

Larry didn't need a pep talk to get him motivated. The letter, burned in his mind, would drive him on for months. When he felt himself slacking off, he'd take it out and read it again.

Chapter 14

There was no quick fix for what ailed Regina. Antidepressants had about the same effect on her system as a handful of M&Ms.

Deep down in her psyche, where Thorazine couldn't touch, she harbored a great sadness. In the lockdown ward at Agnew State Hospital for the mentally ill, Regina was one of a few women with a private room. It had become necessary to lock her in at night because in the open ward she would go from bed to bed, waking up the other patients, demanding they say "I love you." Then she would shout, "Right back at you," loud enough to wake the whole ward.

The real trouble started when some patients, irritated at being disturbed, told her to go to hell and leave them alone. Then the slaps and curses could be heard all over the ward. Regina usually won the physical altercations because she felt that her *work* was important. "I love you—right back at you" had been her last conversation with Larry, and she had to keep it alive, keep it *real*. Anyone who disagreed was the enemy trying to take her love away, and she fought them with the strength of three strong men.

For six long years, Regina stayed the same. Medication that helped other patients, Haldol and Millaril, rolled off her like water off a duck's back. Dennis was eleven and Thompson six and a half; and in all that time, as close as Agnew was to Palo Alto, Regina had not seen her boys.

"They're too young to go out there," Mrs. Hines said. "It might mess them up for life to see their mother in that condition."

Thompson didn't care; he didn't know his mother anyway. He spent all his free time watching "Superman" on television, walking like Superman and talking like Superman. Every night he went to bed in his Superman pajamas. Every morning he ate his cereal out of a bowl with Superman in the bottom, an idea Aunt Cynthia had come up with to get him to eat all his breakfast.

Dennis, on the other hand, remembered his mother and everything about her, the good things and the bad.

He remembered his father too.

When Dennis was almost five, he'd asked his Aunt Cynthia to buy him a reading course, *Hooked on Phonics.* The course came with its own little record player. When his grandpa thought he was sleeping, Dennis was playing his phonic records. At age six and a half he was reading the newspaper to himself.

One day at the school library, Dennis discovered some small records. He checked one out just to see if his little record player could handle it. Although a little scratchy, the voice had come through loud and clear in Spanish: "*De nada*...means it's nothing, *si*...means yes, *Dios*...means God, *Como esta*...means how are you...."

Dennis was so thrilled, he checked out every Spanish record that would fit his little player. In seven months, he was talking fluent Spanish with the Mexican children. To his delight, Dennis discovered there was a record somewhere for almost everything; all he had to do was find it.

His second grade teacher told his grandparents that Dennis was her class liaison, her teacher's aide.

On her days off, Aunt Cynthia taught Dennis to play the black shiny Grand Piano that she had "worked her fingers to the bone," to pay for. At Christmas and other holidays, Dennis played the piano for his class programs and plays. The teachers and other adults adored him, but all the children resented him, called him a "brown-noser" and a "suck-up."

Once in fourth grade, when Dennis was playing basketball with some foul-mouthed boys, Dennis told them, "You know, profanity is the sign of a poor vocabulary."

The team didn't like it, but one boy in particular didn't have the verbal skills to strike back, and so he attacked Dennis personally. "Well, you ain't got no mama and no daddy either, so I guess you was really found in the cabbage patch, huh?"

Dennis didn't let things like that upset him. He knew what he was about. He had his grandma, his grandpa, and Aunt Cynthia, who was a better mother than some of the other kids' *real* parents. Most of all he had his little brother, Thompson. "Friends" could go take a flying leap in the ocean as far as he was concerned.

He had goals and plans to carry out. One was to someday find a cure for his mother. The other was to kill his father.

Chapter 15

Columbia was a tough law school to get into, and once you got in, it was tough to get out of with a degree. One reason for that was the tuition—twenty-nine thousand dollars a year. Most Negroes just didn't have that kind of money and no way to get it.

Another reason Columbia was so tough to get out of was the grade-point average. Lawrence needed a 3.70 to get in. He fought hard to maintain and exceed that average. Upon completion, he was the only Negro left in his class.

Hope Henshaw didn't even try to hide her tears when they called her boy's name and announced him third in the top ten graduates with a grade-point average of 3.97.

She cried openly as she watched Lawrence fulfill her lifelong dream, for himself, for his dead father and stepfather, and for her. Now she could die happy.

After seven long years, the state hospital called to say that Regina could come home for a visit. It seemed they had tried a new medication called Lithium on her, and it seemed to be just what she needed. It worked so well, Regina was almost back to her old self.

Everyone hugged and kissed her, told her how good she looked, but Dennis thought she looked older than Grandma Hines. To make bad matters a whole lot worse, she had called him *Larry* three times in one day.

Dennis knew that he looked a lot like his father: he had the same red hair, big ears, and shocking green eyes in a brown face, but he was still a kid, taller than some boys at eleven and a half, but anybody could see that he was just a kid. How could his mother even think he could be Larry—that big ole mean creep!

It upset Dennis so much that he began to avoid her.

Thompson, once he warmed up to her, spent hours sitting at Regina's knees, telling her stories about Superman and how he wanted to be just like him. Regina, in turn, told Thompson stories about her childhood. Dennis eavesdropped, but stayed out of sight.

One day Dennis overheard his mother telling Thompson about her favorite television show *Laverne and Shirley* who lived in a stoop in Brooklyn, New York. For entertainment they watched for green shoes to walk by their only window, flush with the sidewalk.

"All they could see was the shoes and a little bit of leg," she said. "Then their friend Squiggy would run up the steps to get a look at the whole person. They always had red hair. 'Didn't I tell you?' Squiggy would say, 'Only redheads have the nerve to wear green shoes!' And they all had a wonderful laugh."

Dennis was crouched behind the door, listening. Hearing that story brought to mind the very first time he'd seen his father hit his mommy. There had been yelling and tears and blood on her face.

Hate rose up in his eleven-year-old chest so fierce that he found it hard to breathe. *I hate him for what he did to us,* he thought. *I hate him for hitting my mommy and making her go crazy. I really hate him for being mean to me and Thompson. Someday when I'm bigger, I'll figure out a way to kill that creep.*

Dennis kept a paper in his shoe with a list of ways to kill his father on it. When he read about something clever or saw something good in the movies that just might work for him, he took off his shoe and wrote it on the list. At the top was an idea he'd gotten from an old Alfred Hitchcock mystery magazine.

1. Stab with ice dagger—evidence will melt and leave no trace.

2. Fine ground hair in tea or coffee—will plug kidneys, but kill slow.

3. Oleander flower brewed in coffeepot—will kill in seconds.

4. Six bullets to the head with a .38—swift sure kill.

The list was short, but he was always on the lookout for things to add to it.

Regina had been home from Agnew for a whole week when her father started coughing and couldn't stop. When her mother came to the bedroom to give her the noon pills, she told her, "Regina, I may have to take your father to the doctor. Will you be okay here with Thompson until I get back?"

"Of course," Regina said, "we have fun together."

"All right then, I won't be long. Dennis is at the library; he'll be back after a while. Your Aunt Cynthia gets off at three-thirty; she'll be home by four, but I don't expect to be gone that long. Are you sure you'll be okay?"

"Sure, I'm sure, Mama. What can happen?"

"Well, okay then, honey; see you soon."

Thompson was running around the house with a big beach towel pinned around his neck for a cape, pretending to be Superman. When he got thirsty, he poured himself a glass of milk and went to his mother's room.

"Hey, Mommy, what you doing in here?"

"Oh, just kicking back, son. What you doing?" The medicine made her mellow.

"Oh, just playing Superman, Mommy."

"You never get tired of that, do you, Thompson?" she asked.

"No, Mommy, 'cause someday I'm going to be just like Superman. Do you think I could fly?"

"Sure," Regina told her son, "you can do anything you want to do if you put your mind to it and try hard enough."

Thompson finished his milk and stood up. "Well, I'm going back outside to play, Mommy; see you later."

"Okay, Superman," she ruffled his hair, "see you later."

Thompson went back outside; he took a couple of turns around the house to warm up. When he thought he was ready, he began climbing up the fire escape. It took him a long time; the rungs were slick, and his legs were short. He kept slipping, but he finally managed to reach the top. He sat down to rest a minute, to put his mind to it. When he was ready, he stood up, adjusted his cape, spread his arms exactly like Superman, and flew off Aunt Cynthia's three-story house. His head hit the trunk of the old oak tree in the backyard and split open like a melon.

Aunt Cynthia was the first to come home. She went straight to Regina's room. "How you doing, honey? Where is everybody?"

"Fine, Aunt Cyn. Mama took Daddy to the doctor. Dennis is at the library, and Thompson is outside playing."

"Okay then," Cynthia said. "I'm going to grab a quick shower."

Dennis was the next to come home. He went straight to the kitchen and poured himself a glass of milk; and since he didn't see his grandmother anywhere, he snagged a couple of tea cakes before dinner. He knew his mother was in her room; she didn't walk around a lot because the medicine made her walk like Lurch on the Addams Family. Dennis knew because he'd looked it up and read about the side effects. He decided to just poke his head in, say a quick "Hi," and escape to his room, 'cause if she called him *Larry* one more time, he was going to *explode*—self-destruct right before her eyes!

It was getting close to six o'clock. It was time for Regina to have her medication. The doctor at Agnew had been firm, "Every six hours on the dot; don't ever miss a dose."

She was getting antsy, clenching and unclenching her hands, pumping her left foot up and down like a bellows fanning a fire.

Then Dennis stuck his head in the door and said, "Hi, Mom."

He was halfway down the hall when Regina whispered, "Hello, Larry, I love you."

Mrs. Hines came home alone. Her eyes were red and swollen. She had cried all her tears out at the hospital. "Your grandpa is gone," she told a wide-eyed Dennis.

"What happened?" Cynthia asked, shocked.

"Well, by the time I got him to the doctors, he was gasping for breath, chain-stoking the doctor called it.

They rushed him right over to the hospital, but the nurse said she couldn't find his pulse, and he didn't have no blood pressure to speak of. They called a code blue, and everybody came running in with bottles and electrical stuff to shock him with, but I wouldn't let 'em. He was gone anyway. I told them to leave him alone and let him rest.

Where is Thompson?"

"He's outside playing," Cynthia said.

"This late?" Mrs. Hines said. "Go get him, Dennis; he knows it's past time to come in and wash up for dinner. I don't know what I'm gonna do with that boy. Him and his Superman."

After Dennis left to look for Thompson, Mrs. Hines turned to Cynthia. "Will you go break the news about her dad to Regina? You're a nurse; I'm sure you can do it much better than I can."

When Cynthia was gone from the kitchen, Mrs. Hines put her head in both hands. Lordy, she was tired. Dinner would come right out of a can tonight. She didn't give a thought to Regina's medication.

The screams rose up at the same time, one from Cynthia in Regina's room, the other from Dennis in the backyard. Mrs. Hines didn't know which way to run. In a split second she decided to go see about the children since Regina and Cynthia were both adults.

When she reached the backyard, Dennis was kneeling over his brother, swatting gnats and flies away from his busted head.

"What's the matter with him, Dennis?" Mrs. Hines called before she was close enough to see for herself.

"His head is broken, Grandma. His head is broken wide open!" Dennis babbled.

Aunt Cynthia had heard the screams too, and she abandoned Regina for what sounded like something more urgent going on in the backyard. She fell to her knees at the same time that her sister, Lois Hines did. After a quick assessment of the situation, she barked orders at Dennis, "Go call 911, Dennis; then call Mrs. Kim next door and ask her to please come over. Tell her it's an emergency."

After Dennis ran for help, Aunt Cynthia examined little Thompson's body for signs of life. She didn't try to start CPR; anybody could tell that rigor mortis had set in— hours and hours ago.

From the backdoor, Regina watched the paramedics cover her baby boy up with a black plastic sheet and drive slowly down the hill with the emergency lights blinking. Aunt Cynthia rode with them.

There is really no reason to hurry, a sane corner of her mind reasoned, *he's already dead, so why turn on the sirens and have people pulling over to let them pass? A thousand years won't bring him back to me.*

And she shuffled back to her room, looked in the mirror, balled up her fist, and hit herself in the right eye so hard that it doubled in size in an instant.

"You're a bad ugly person, Regina," she said to her image in the mirror. "You was a bad wife, and you are a bad mother." With that said, she picked up the little wooden music box and slammed it into her open mouth to the tune of Clair de Lune. Teeth and blood splattered the white French Provencal dresser.

"Now there; that's just what you deserve," she said, while searching around with her left eye for something sharp. When she spied a ball point pen, she seized it with both hands, sat back on the quilted coverlet of the queen-sized bed, and drove the point into the tender flesh of her thighs, again and again.

Later that evening, when Mrs. Hines finally thought about giving Regina her medication, the room resembled a slaughterhouse.

Prior to her leave of absence, Regina's diagnosis across the top of her chart, had taken up half a line: Major Depression, Mild Manic, Anxiety, Catatonic, Combative.

Upon her return to the hospital, the doctor added: Highly Agitated, Self-Abusive, Early Dementia, Major Manic Depression, and Poor Risk.

She had to be locked up and watched with both arms restrained to prevent her from biting herself. Regina was beyond Lithium, the drug that had once helped her. She was a raving maniac, out of control.

The family's request for a one-day leave so Regina could attend the double funeral of her son and her father was denied.

The older children came to their father's funeral: Gordon, Cecilia, and Bonnie. They didn't know about Thompson until they got there. They didn't know their sister, Regina, either, except for letters and a few childhood snapshots. When Mrs. Hines told them the story about how Thompson died, they all shook their heads.

"His ticket was punched," Gordon said, "it was just his time to go."

Cecilia said, "That's why we should live each day as if it was our last; long life is not promised to any of us."

"Yes," Bonnie put in, "there's just as many short graves as there are long ones."

When Mrs. Hines told them of Regina's forced marriage and of her current situation, the conversation got more heated.

"Papa shouldn't have made her marry that joker," Gordon said. "She would a been better off without him."

Bonnie was looking intently into her mother's eyes when she said softly, "You know, Mama, sometimes we don't pay enough attention to the laws of God. Why do you think he made menopause? It means *stop, pause, men and women*. Don't have children after forty-five years of age."

"Yeah, Mama," said Cecilia, "you're lucky Regina wasn't *born* retarded."

Aunt Cynthia broke it up by reminding her nieces and nephew that her sister didn't need a lecture, but rather love and compassion in her time of sorrow.

The bouquet they bought his grandpa was the biggest Dennis had ever seen. It covered the whole casket. Thompson had a lot of flowers too. Every kid in the first grade brought a vase filled with daisies and sunflowers, Thompson's favorite. Dennis sneaked Thompson's Superman cereal bowl in under his jacket and put it in his coffin. He pushed it way down out of sight. Dennis knew that was the only thing Thompson needed to take him into heaven.

After perfunctory hugs and kisses, everyone went away, leaving Mrs. Hines, Aunt Cynthia, and Dennis at the open graves.

"Well, loves, let's go home now," Aunt Cynthia said gently.

"Why?" Dennis cried, "they're not buried yet."

"Well, Dennis, they don't let us watch while the dirt is being shoveled in on them. It traumatizes people. More than one person has died just watching their loved ones be covered up with dirt."

"Well, I won't die," Dennis said. "I wanna see 'em do it." He was worried about the cereal bowl being discovered.

When the coffins were lowered and covered up to Dennis' satisfaction, they went home.

Chapter 16

Lawrence Armstead's name was a household word. He knew that he was the richest lawyer in New York because he made it his business to find out. He was feared and respected in legal circles and hated by every crook who'd had the misfortune to tangle with him in a court of law. Lawrence was a prosecuting attorney, known to put a criminal away. He knew how they thought, could get into their minds because he had a criminal mind himself.

The white criminals called him *Black Armstead*. Over the years, that name got shortened to *The Black Arm*. The crooks of color, out of respect for race, just called him *The Arm*, but they all made plans to do something nasty to him if they ever got out.

Today, he had another blinding headache. He sat at his desk, holding his head in both hands, massaging his temples. He knew he should eat something, but just the thought of his once favorite rare steak with lobster made his stomach queasy.

Lawrence blamed it on the smoke. The last time he'd gone out to eat, the place had been so smoky, you could cut the air with a knife, and the noise had made his headache worse. He'd thrown his own pack of Benson and Hedges in the trash and had gotten out of there.

What I need is a good old-fashioned home-cooked meal, he thought, remembering his mother's pot roast. Lord, how he missed his mama! After ten years, the ache still brought tears to his eyes. He blamed it all on Regina. Because of her, he had wasted precious time while his mama's heart condition grew worse.

Lawrence had tried to make it up to her. He moved her to New York into his penthouse, got a maid to wait on her hand and foot, and hired the best doctors in the nation to fix her heart. But they said she had waited too long, and the damage was done. They had put his mama on the list for a heart transplant, but she had died before they could find one.

Lawrence didn't hear his secretary come in. He jerked at the sound of her voice. "Ilene, didn't I tell you I didn't want to be disturbed!"

"I know, Mr. Armstead, but Mr. Melvin Belli is on the line. He would like to know if you could come to another one of his weddings."

"Tell him of course, Ilene, when is it?"

"Two weeks from tomorrow, sir."

"Well, you tell him I'll see him then and to have me a date lined up."

Of course he would go. Melvin was one of his best friends. He'd learned so much from him over the years, tricks that couldn't be taught in school.

When he looked up again, Ilene was still standing there. "Well, what are you waiting for, go tell him!"

"I just wanted to say that you don't look so good, Mr. Armstead. Is it the headache again? I wish you would let me make an appointment for you with Doctor Gerald Terry. And if you're going to San Francisco, you'll need a new suit; the others are all too big." Frowning, she turned on her heels and went back to her desk.

Lawrence watched her go. She was a good secretary, the best, and he knew she cared about him. Once he had peeked over her shoulder at the title of an article she was reading in the *Essence Magazine.* "How to chase a man until *he* catches *you.*" Well, he didn't intend to catch anybody, no matter how hard they chased *him.* He had too much to hide.

Once he had made the mistake of dating a widow from Queens who was known to get her man. "If I can't get him, he's either *gay or dead*" was her motto. Lawrence had a lot of fun with her, until she got serious. Then he broke it off.

Rejected, she had spread the word around that he was gay. Lawrence didn't care; he knew what he was.

If he ever would get married again, he'd pick Ilene or someone like her: pretty, smart, and sensitive. Yesterday, when he'd lost his case in court, Ilene had actually cried for him. Hell, he had cried for himself. He should have won that case. But he'd been so tired, in spite of drinking half a bottle of Geritol Tonic, and his head just wouldn't let up, even after taking a handful of Tylenol.

He had been slow, missed something, and the young defense attorney stepped into the gap and drove his point home. He had lost; the criminal walked.

Lawrence's motto "You can't lose with the stuff I use" was flung at him when he met up with the baby-faced defense attorney in the men's room.

"Well, old man, looks like your *stuff* is slipping a bit." Lawrence wanted to hit him, but he was too tired to raise his hand.

Chapter 17

Flying was not one of Lawrence Armstead's favorite things to do. But this time, he didn't worry about the damn thing falling; he intended to get some rest. And if it fell, well then he would just rest forever.

He crawled into the plush seat and hit the recline button. His intentions were to sleep all the way from New York to San Francisco.

It felt as if he had just closed his eyes, when the stewardess tapped him on the shoulder. "Dinner is served, Mr. Armstead. Would you like to sit up and let out your tray?"

"*No*, I would not *like*," he snapped, irritated because she woke him up. "Just bring me three packs of those toasted almonds and don't bother me again until you see the skyline of Frisco." Nuts were good for you, were they not? And it didn't take forever and a day to eat them. Probably had more nourishment than that plate of cordon bleu, and you didn't have to cut 'em with a knife.

Melvin Belli had a stretch-limo waiting for him at San Francisco International Airport. He rode in comfort and style all the way to the Mark Hopkins Hotel on Nob Hill.

Lawrence was accustomed to luxury, but his room on the fifth floor of the grand old hotel took his breath away. Old Melvin knew how to do things *right*.

Nob Hill was just waking up, and Lawrence felt pretty good himself after sleeping all night on his flight. Maybe he would go out later for some seafood and walk the streets a little. He loved the feel and smell of the city. But first, he would take a bath.

The tub was big enough for him to walk across, all enclosed in Plexiglas in case one decided to shower instead. Lawrence filled the tub with steaming hot water and slid beneath the bubbles. There was no hurry; he had all day. Nobody else on earth would think of getting married at night, but Melvin Belli. He felt glad the reception would be held right here in the Mark Hopkins ballroom, where his date would be waiting. Lawrence found himself hoping she wouldn't be a chatterbox. He didn't feel like listening to a bunch of polite hot air. He knew for sure that she would be tall and beautiful. They always were because Melvin knew what he liked. He was thinking after a few dances and some polite amenities, he would escape back to his room and try out that canopy bed with the velvet patch-work quilt. Alone.

A ringing telephone woke him up. Lawrence jumped out of the cold water, reached for a bath towel, and in his haste, bumped his forearm on the Plexiglas shower enclosure.

"Damn," he muttered, "how could I go to sleep taking a bath?" He padded naked across the room and picked up the receiver. "Armstead here."

"Hey, old buddy, where the hell are you? Things are going to start popping here pretty soon, and we haven't seen hide nor hair of you!"

Lawrence tried to make his voice sound light, "Sorry 'bout that, Mel. Guess I dozed off there for a minute, long flight, you know. See you in a few."

Where had the day gone? Lawrence got dressed in record time. He didn't notice the large bruise until he started to pull on his shirt. "Oh, wow, where did that come from?" He muttered, examining his arm. The whole inside of his forearm was black and blue.

Then Lawrence remembered hitting it on the tub enclosure, "I must have been really groggy; didn't think I hit it *that* hard." He was talking to himself again.

It was a stellar affair. The food was wonderful; Lawrence actually ate some. His date was all that he had imagined; she looked as if she had just stepped out of the pages of a magazine. In fact, she *had* just stepped out of the pages of the newspaper since she was I. Magnin's top black model.

Lawrence found himself wishing he could work up enough energy to take her to his room. That dress alone, what little there was of it, made him catch his breath. There was no back at all, and the front came up just high enough to cover her perky breasts. The skirt was short and full, designed to show off a lot of leg. He decided the little thing was being held up by gravity and pulled her closer. He was trying to get a better look down that cleavage, when her scream split the air so loud, it hurt his ears.

The band stopped playing in mid-note. Couples stood with their arms around each other staring at him.

"What the hell's the matter?" he asked the girl, who was backing away, bumping into other people.

"You're bleeding on me, you son of a bitch! You're bleeding right down in my dress, I got a bra full of *blood*!"

Now this was news to Lawrence; he didn't think she had on a bra. His date took a step back toward him, and sure enough, the top of her little dress was filled with blood. Lawrence could see it start to seep through the delicate pink fabric. It had happened so fast; he still had his arms in the dancing position, holding air, when someone put a white handkerchief in his hand.

"Here man, put this to your nose, you're bleeding all over yourself!" Lawrence looked down and saw that he too was covered with blood. He didn't care about the shirt or the suit; they could be replaced, but his favorite black tie was ruined. His mother had given that tie to him. Lawrence started to cry. Someone took his other hand and led him toward the men's room. Just before the door closed, he heard his date scream, "If you have AIDS, I'm suing your behind; I don't care if you are a lawyer!"

Melvin Belli made the call to 911 himself. Paramedics arrived in fewer than five minutes. Mr. Belli was not someone to get on the wrong side of. After they had stopped the nosebleed, paramedics offered to transport Lawrence to San Francisco General Hospital. Melvin nixed that idea and instructed his chauffeur to drive Lawrence to Stanford Emergency in his private limousine.

Lawrence owed Melvin a lot. He fully intended to settle up as soon as he got back to New York City.

After answering five pages of questions about his past history, the emergency room doctors gave Lawrence every test known to man. Then they started an intravenous drip to hydrate his body and piggy-backed it with a pint of blood.

After the second pint of packed blood cells, Lawrence felt so well that he thought he could go back to the party.

"I don't think you'll be leaving us tonight, Mr. Armstead," a cute little nurse told him. "We already have a bed for you. Better for you to stay here until all your test results come back."

When the transportation orderly rolled him to his room, Lawrence read the sign over the double doors, "Oncology Unit."

After two days, Lawrence was still watching the clear fluid drip into his arm. His appetite had come back; he was cleaning his food tray at every meal. "Why do I need more of that stuff?" he asked the night nurse when she tiptoed in to hang a new bottle.

"To keep your electrolytes in balance," she told him.

"What's wrong with my electrolytes? I eat all my food. I even eat my snacks."

"Well, now that's good to hear. This is only normal saline," she said, backtracking. "We need to keep a line open in case of emergency."

"What kind of emergency?" he asked, interrogating her.

"Ah, in case you need some more blood, for example. Then we won't have to stick you again." And she was gone from the room before he could ask any more questions.

The next morning, when Lawrence was supposed to be flying back to New York, he was getting a complete bed bath by a friendly nurse's aide. "You're going to have company this morning, Mr. Armstead. You might want to shave," the nurses aide informed him. "I'd be glad to do it for you, or I can bring you some warm water and a safety razor if you'd rather do it yourself. Your choice."

"You bring the equipment, Tim. I think I can manage." Lawrence was just finishing up when they filed into his room, introducing themselves as they came.

"Morning, Mr. Armstead, my name is Doctor Julio Fisher from Blood Cancer Research, and this is my assistant Doctor Jerry De Jesus."

Lawrence nodded. They looked like twins, or brothers, both with horn-rimmed glasses, white lab coats, and bald. The next two, he already knew: Doctor Jesse Davidson, the oncology doctor who looked in on him from time to time, and his head nurse, Joyce Jones. The last person to enter was quick to say that she was not a doctor. Her name was Wanda Martinez, and she was from the Leukemia and Lymphoma Society. They all carried clipboards.

Doctor Davidson spoke first. "Mr. Armstead, we have bad news for you."

Lawrence had already figured that out for himself. "Let me have it, Doctor." He tried to sound upbeat, but a cold dread was spreading inside him.

"You have leukemia, a cancer of the blood."

"What can you do about it?" Lawrence addressed the whole group.

Doctor Fisher answered. "We have no cure—yet, but we are working hard to find one."

"And that is where I come in," Wanda Martinez said, smiling, "Leukemia and Lymphoma Society work tirelessly to raise money for research, new treatments and cures."

Lawrence got hope. "If it's money you need to fix me, I have plenty of that. How much do you need?"

Doctor De Jesus took over, "We certainly would appreciate a donation, Mr. Armstead, but we can't promise you a cure. We have found drugs to slow the disease if detected early: Chemotherapy being one. But in your case, you ignored the signs and symptoms."

"Why didn't you seek medical help when you first experienced chronic fatigue—that is, when you first began to feel weak and tired all the time?" Doctor Davidson asked.

Lawrence answered, "Because I thought I was weak and tired from not eating. You see, I lost my appetite when the headaches started."

"How long has it been since the headaches started, Mr. Armstead?" Doctor Fisher wanted to know.

Lawrence was thoughtful for a few seconds. "Oh, five, maybe six months ago."

Doctor Davidson was looking at him closely. "And in all that time you never thought to seek medical help?"

Lawrence tried to defend himself. "Hey, I am a prosecuting attorney, folks; headaches, joint pain, loss of appetite, and weakness are part of the trade sometimes. On one case, I was up three days and nights, running on caffeine and eating sardines right out of the can. I was tired and weak; my head was aching, but I won my case. See what I mean?"

"Well, I'm afraid it has gone on too long," doctor Davidson said. "The only treatment that *may* benefit you now would be a bone marrow transplant. Anything else is out of the question. You've waited too long, I'm sorry to say."

Lawrence couldn't quite believe what he had heard. "You said I'll need a *what*, doctor?"

"I said you will need a bone marrow transplant. Is there anyone in your family that we could approach for testing? The cells must be an exact match with yours. How about your mother?"

"No mother." Lawrence shook his head. "She passed on three years after I finished law school."

"What did she die from, Mr. Armstead?" Doctor Fisher asked.

"Her heart was blocked." Lawrence still had to grit his teeth to keep from crying—after all these years.

"Heart block?" Doctor De Jesus pressed him. "They can do bypass with their eyes closed now. Why did your mother die from heart blockage?"

"Because," Larry said, tears shining in his eyes, "she refused to have the operation until I got out of law school. She wanted to live to see her dream come true, and there are so many risks with heart surgery. My mother made the decision to wait. I was working as hard as anyone could, studying hard, getting good grades. And that was not easy because I went home as often as I could to check on her, which resulted in work to be made up for the days I had missed.

"One day I left school to see about my mother, and she was at the doctor's when I got there. While she was gone, these people knocked on our door. I tried to tell them that Mama wasn't home, that she was sick and had gone to see her doctor, but they wouldn't listen.

"The man had a shotgun and a minister along with his teenage daughter, who they said I had gotten pregnant."

"Well, did you do it?" Doctor De Jesus asked.

"Yes, I guess so," Lawrence admitted. "The girl already had a three-year-old son."

"Yours?" Wanda Martinez wanted to know.

"Yes, mine!" Lawrence snapped. He was getting tired of their questions. "The girl got pregnant every time I touched her. They forced me to marry her right there on our front porch, at gunpoint. When Mama came home, I had to tell her that I was married. It almost killed her, right there on the spot, but she hung on. My mama was tough.

"The girl's family knew I was going to school in New York, but not exactly where, so they moved the girl and the kid to Brooklyn and paid the rent for eight months. My own mama sent food money to feed them so that I could stay in school. It was $29,000 a year to keep me at Columbia Law School.

"After the girl had the other baby, we only had six months rent paid up. I tried to get the girl to start looking for a job to pay the rent when the six months ran out. You see, there was no way my mama could afford to pay that rent and keep me in school too. She was already feeding them with part of my stepdad's social security check. All the girl had to do was make enough money to pay the rent. Her father had threatened to kill me if I didn't take care of them, and I believed him because he was dying of some kind of lung sickness and had nothing to lose.

"But the girl wouldn't work. I even got her a job, in a shoe factory, right there in Brooklyn, but she wouldn't go, refused to leave the kids."

Lawrence didn't like the way the group was looking at him.

"To make a long story short, I dropped out of school, took a job in a luggage factory nights so that I could study some in the day time. It was my mother who came up with the idea to just get rid of them, send them to California, and let her folks worry about them. And so I did."

"What is your wife's name, Mr. Armstead?" Doctor Davidson asked, frowning.

"Regina Henshaw. I hated her for what she did to me!"

"What are your sons' names?"

"The oldest is Dennis; the youngest is Thompson Henshaw."

Doctor Davidson was puzzled. "If you are the father, how is it they don't carry your last name?"

Lawrence was getting tired of them. He spoke quickly. "Because I was going in my stepfather's name at that time. I didn't take my real name until I started law school at Columbia. That is how my mother had my life laid out, and I could not deviate from her plans since she was in control of my trust fund." He turned his head away.

Doctor Davidson pulled up a chair and sat down near Lawrence's head. He took his pen and clipboard and prepared to write. "I need the full names of your wife and children, Mr. Armstead. Also their address and telephone number. We need to find a bone marrow match for you quickly; you don't have much time."

Lawrence was ashamed to admit that he didn't know the address or the telephone number of his family, but his fear of death soon overcame that. "I can't tell you the address or the telephone number, doctor; all I know is they live somewhere in Palo Alto, California. Dennis, the oldest, would be finishing up high school this year, if I'm counting right."

There were incredulous looks and whispers from the group around his bed. Doctor Davidson spoke out. "Let me get this straight, Mr. Armstead. You didn't send any child support payments to take care of your boys? Even after you got your trust fund and became rich and famous? You didn't send them anything?"

"No!" Lawrence yelled as loud as his moist lungs would let him. "You people don't understand. I *hated* them for what they did to me and Mama."

"And what was *that*?" Doctor Fisher asked.

"They tried to keep me from getting my education, to keep my mama from realizing her lifelong dream!"

Doctor Fisher wouldn't let it go. "So you blame the *children* for what you and Regina did? You're a *lawyer*, Mr. Armstead; one would expect better from you."

Lawrence was tired of talking about it. "Be that as it may."

"Okay, Mr. Armstead, okay. Can you think of anything else that would expedite our search for the boys?"

Lawrence thought for a moment. "Well, I know they went to Palo Alto, and I seem to remember Regina saying once that she had an aunt who worked at Stanford."

"You mean right here at Stanford University?" Joyce Jones, the head nurse asked.

"I don't know about that, but her first name is Cynthia. I have no idea what her last name might be."

"If she's here at Stanford, we'll find her," Doctor Davidson assured him. "Is your wife's aunt a Negro?"

Larry bristled. "This is a new age, Doctor. We prefer to be called Afro-Americans, if you please."

"With all due respect, Mr. Armstead," Doctor Davidson shot back, "you can call it whatever you want to, but you don't have time to *nit-pick*."

"Do I have *time* to call my secretary in New York?" Lawrence snapped. "I have promises to keep and miles to go before I sleep," he said, toying with his favorite poem by Robert Frost. Those who knew the work smiled. The ones who didn't just thought he was being morbid.

Chapter 18

Doctor Davidson didn't have much trouble finding Cynthia Thompson; she was the only Afro-American working on the fourth floor of Stanford's pain clinic.

He realized that he already knew her. Last Thanksgiving they had sat at the same lunch table, and he'd teased her about eating a sack lunch when everyone else had their plates piled high with turkey and dressing. The conversation flicked across his mind.

"You're eating a peanut butter and jelly sandwich, instead of this glorious turkey dinner? What are you, some kind of vegetarian?"

Cynthia thought that was funny. "No, Doctor, I love meat; I just don't eat anybody's cooking unless I know they washed their hands."

"Aw, come on, nurse," he said, not bothering to look at her name tag, "the heat kills germs."

"Oh, well," she'd said, folding up the brown paper bag, "heat didn't kill that *e-coli* outbreak we had last year. Excuse me, Doctor, gotta run."

Doctor Davidson waited until Cynthia finished instructing a patient, and then he stepped up to her desk. "Hello, Miss Thompson."

"Oh, hi, Doctor," she said, surprised to see him.

"May I have a word with you in private, Miss Thompson?"

"Sure," she said, "room one is empty; why don't I meet you in there in about one minute, and call me Cynthia please."

Doctor Davidson went around the corner to room one and took a seat on the examination table. It was more like five minutes before she came rushing in. "Sorry to keep you waiting," she looked at his name tag, "Doctor Davidson."

"Think nothing of it, Cynthia. I have some personal questions to ask you. I hope you don't mind."

Cynthia tensed; she hoped he wasn't going to ask her for a date. It was her habit not to date outside her race, although the pickings were mighty slim. Men her age were already married, or there was something wrong with them. "Go ahead, Doctor. If it's not too personal, I won't mind."

"Good. Cynthia, do you have a nephew named Dennis Henshaw?"

"Yes, I do," her heart skipped a beat. "Is anything wrong with him?"

"No, no, nothing like that. Do you know your nephew's father, Lawrence Armstead?"

"Oh, you have the wrong Dennis; my nephew's father's name is Larry Henshaw. I've never met him, and I'm not sure I want to from what I've heard about him. This Lawrence Armstead you speak of is a very famous Negro lawyer in New York. Everybody knows about him. They call him *The Arm*, you know, short for Armstead. He's in all the magazines and newspapers."

Doctor Davidson shook his head. "Right now, he's downstairs in room 314 dying of leukemia, Cynthia. He said he had two sons, Dennis and Thompson, in Palo Alto. I believe we're talking about the same ones..."

Cynthia cut him off. "Thompson is dead, Doctor. He died a long time ago, and Dennis is in school."

"Sorry to hear that, Cynthia. How did the child die?"

"He fell, Doctor, fell off the roof."

"Tragic! Is Dennis eighteen yet?"

"Not until Christmas, Doctor, why?"

"We need him to give his father a bone marrow transplant—that is, if he's a match. It's the man's only chance; he has no other relatives. There's not much time left. We must test Dennis and do it quickly."

"Why is Larry going around calling himself Lawrence Armstead?" Cynthia had her doubts.

"It's a long story, Cynthia. I'll try to give you the gist of it. Then, I hope you will help me contact your nephew."

When Doctor Davidson finished, Cynthia had no doubts Larry was indeed Regina's husband and Dennis' father. She went with Doctor Davidson to the school.

Dennis was dissecting a frog. Although the principal said it was an emergency, he finished his assignment, put away his tools, and washed his hands before going to the office. It was his habit not to let anything interfere with his 4.0 grade-point average.

Chapter 19

When he saw Aunt Cynthia with a strange man, he felt apprehensive and hoped nothing had happened to his grandmother. Aunt Cynthia put her arms around his shoulder and put his mind at ease. "It's about your father, Dennis."

Dennis jerked away from her. "What about him?" If they had come to tell him the joker was dead, he could have stayed in class.

"He's right here at Stanford, and he's very, very sick, Dennis."

"Leukemia." Doctor Davidson took over. "He needs a bone marrow transplant right away, and you are his only hope. We need you to come to the hospital and let us test you. If you are a match with your father, we hope you will be willing to let us do a bone marrow transplant from you to him in order to save his life."

"Will you do it, Dennis?" Aunt Cynthia pleaded. "It won't hurt. I'll go to the hospital with you and stay right by your side. If we go right away, you won't miss a day of school."

Dennis pretended to be thinking about it. He knew all about bones, from the periosteum to the yellow marrow to the medullary cavity and the red marrow cavities. He knew all about transplants too. And he knew biopsy wasn't painful.

"What is he doing in California?" Dennis asked, wasting precious time.

"It's a long story, Dennis; and we intend to tell it to you, but right now, we need to know if you'll agree to have the bone marrow test?" Doctor Davidson asked.

"Oh, yes!" Dennis said, faking enthusiasm. "Let's go!"

The biopsy was a snap. Dennis thought he could have done it to himself if he could have reached back there.

All through the preparation and procedure, Aunt Cynthia held tight to his hand while telling him the story of how Larry had changed his name and become one of the most famous lawyers of color in the nation.

While my mother was rotting away in the nut house, Dennis thought, *he was rolling in dough. When I needed a pair of rain boots to keep my feet dry, he had enough money to have me chauffeured to school in a limousine. When my little brother died and my grandmother had to borrow money to bury him, Larry had enough money to bury half the people in Stanford. He was rolling in dough, but he didn't see fit to help his own flesh and blood, and, oh God, how I hate him for that.*

"Yes, Aunt Cynthia," he said, "I think it's wonderful that my father has attained such heights. I feel honored to be the one to help him." *Into hell!* his mind added.

Grandma Hines was upset. "Your grandpa would turn over in his grave if he knew that you was risking your life for that no-good man, Dennis."

Dennis smiled and hugged her. "Don't you worry none, Grandma. I ain't risking my life or anything else. Grandpa can rest easy."

The results came in by phone before the lab slips got delivered to the ward clerk. "It's a match. It's a match!" echoed up and down the corridors of the third floor.

The place had a festive atmosphere; everybody was pulling for Lawrence until Dennis walked down the hall, looking for room 314. He gave everyone such black looks that they moved out of his way.

When he entered the room, his father was sleeping. Dennis checked out the profile. He wished he didn't look so much like this creep.

Sensing someone near, Lawrence's lids flew open. "Oh, hello, son. I hope I didn't keep you waiting long. I just dozed off for a minute."

Dennis let three beats go by while Lawrence looked him over. "We look a lot alike, huh, son?"

Dennis squared his shoulders. "My name is Dennis Henshaw, and you may call me Dennis.

"Okay, Dennis, permit me to say that you are a fine looking man."

"Thank you, Larry, permission granted."

Heavy silence hung in the room until Lawrence asked, "Did you hear about the test results, Dennis?"

"I heard; that's the only reason why I'm here."

"Okay, son, I mean Dennis, when do we start?"

Dennis took his time. "When do you start being a father or when do I start being a son? Which one do you mean?"

"The ball is in your court," Lawrence said, "you tell me."

"Wellll...," Dennis said slowly, "I can tell you from jump street that I'm not in any hurry. How about you?"

Lawrence studied his son's face. "So that's how it's going to be, huh? What do you want in return for my life, Dennis?"

The room was quiet for a long time before Dennis broke the silence. "Your checkbook for starters."

"And what do you want my checkbook for, Dennis?"

Dennis rolled his eyes at him. "My little brother died a long time ago, and my grandmother had to take out a loan to pay for his funeral expenses because we had no insurance, you see. I want you to write out a check for the full amount, plus interest, payable to Lois Hines."

"Okay, Dennis, look over there in my coat pocket and give me my check..."

"That's not all!" Dennis cut him off. "My mama is wasting away in a state hospital, crazy as a loon because of what you did to her. I have not computed the cost yet, but I'll let you know tomorrow. You being a lawyer and all, I'm sure you'll understand when I include pain and suffering."

Lawrence didn't care; all he wanted was for this boy to give him some bone marrow. "Whatever you say, Dennis."

"Good," Dennis smiled for the first time since entering the room, "because I just remembered you owe my mother a ticket on the train back to New York.

"Now, Larry, it doesn't amount to much in dollars and cents, but it's one of the things that drove her over the edge. I'm afraid you will have to pay for that."

Lawrence was growing tired of this kid. "Look here, I get the picture, and money is no object. I have more money than you have ever seen or ever *will* see! So don't talk to me about money; it insults me."

"All right then, Mr. Armstead, I mean Larry, since money insults you, let us talk about emotions. My mother is pining away for you in Agnew State Hospital, less than an hour from here. I want you to go to her and make things right."

Lawrence sat straight up; the extra exertion made him wheeze. "I can't *do* that! My doctors won't let me leave this hospital. I'm waiting here in this bed for a bone marrow transplant. *Your bone marrow*, and you're playing games, wasting valuable time!"

"It's your time and my bone marrow," Dennis shot back. "If you want it, you'll find a way to do what I say."

He fished in his pocket for a piece of paper. "Here's my phone number. When you've worked it out, call me. I'll go out there with you."

Without saying another word, he turned and left the room.

Fifteen hours later, Dennis got the call. "I'm ready," Lawrence croaked.

"That's just fine," Dennis said. "I'll pick you up in twenty minutes in Aunt Cynthia's car."

Chapter 20

The grounds at Agnew were beautiful and green. Well- tended flowerbeds bloomed around the wide lawn. It looked serene and tranquil. Inside the women's ward, chaos reigned.

Regina was locked in her room, raising hell because she didn't like what they had for lunch. She poured the vegetable soup out onto the cement floor and then pulled handfuls of her hair out and threw them on top of the puddle. "Pig slop. Pig slop. Pig slop," she chanted like a mantra.

When the psychiatric technician unlocked the door for her visitors, Lawrence thought he was looking at a giant spider on the floor and jumped back. Dennis caught him in the back with a sharp elbow. "Get on in there and see what you've done to my *mama*!"

Lawrence stepped over the mess and looked at Regina. For once in his life, he felt sorrow. Not really for Regina, but the feeling one gets upon seeing a car accident where bodies are left broken and mangled—sorrow for the situation.

"Hello, Regina," he whispered.

Thinking for sure that she was hallucinating again, Regina raised her right arm and bit a chunk out of it.

"No! Mom!" Dennis cried, pinning her arms behind her back. "It's Larry, Mom; don't do that! He came to see you!"

Still too much for Regina to comprehend, she walked around Larry, looking at his shiny shoes, the expensive suit, and finally at his face. Reaching out to touch him, she croaked, "Larry, is it really you?"

Shocked at the look of her, Lawrence found it difficult to utter a simple "yes." There was no hair at all on the right side of her head. One big solitary tooth stuck out of her swollen gums like a witch's fang. The right eyelid didn't work at all, but the left lid fluttered nonstop, as if to make up for its partner's paralysis. Along with the fresh bite, Regina's arms were covered with old scars, healing discolored bruises, and blood from the recent attack on herself.

Lawrence thought the only thing that remained of the old Regina was the light brown color of her left eye blinking at him out of a scratched moon face. If he hadn't known for sure that it was Regina, she would have scared him.

Dennis shoved him from behind. "Get over there and hug her!" Larry put one arm around Regina and hugged her shoulder.

"Hug her tight, you sorry creep," Dennis screamed at Lawrence. "Kiss her too, kiss her until I tell you to stop."

When the housekeeping department came to clean up the mess in Regina's room, Dennis ended it. "Okay, you can stop now. Tell her you love her, and we'll go."

"I love you, Regina," Larry said, in a voice that didn't sound at all like Lawrence 'The Arm' Armstead.

Regina was infused with happiness. She hopped around her room singing, "Right back at you," for days.

On the way back to the hospital, Lawrence didn't want to talk. Tired and repulsed didn't come close to describing how he felt, but Dennis kept after him.

"You did well back there; Mama will be very happy for a long time. Thank you."

"What next?" Lawrence asked, sensing more to come.

"I was going to wait until tomorrow to talk to you about Thompson, but I guess this is just as good a time as any. May save you a few hours on your life."

Lawrence had had it. "What about Thompson? You told me he was dead! Why do we have to talk about it anymore?"

"Because, you are responsible for Thompson's death."

"How?" Lawrence whispered, unbelievingly, "I wasn't anywhere near California when he died. What the hell are you talking about, boy?"

Dennis took his time, driving thoughtfully. "If Thompson had had a father to look up to, instead of Superman, he wouldn't have been trying to fly off the roof."

"Sorry," Lawrence muttered, too tired to deny the horrible accusations.

"Not as sorry as you're gonna be," Dennis promised, as they pulled up beside the well-lit building. "Thompson was my little brother *and* my best friend. You get out and think on that for a while." Dennis let Lawrence make his own way back to room 314. It was getting late, and he had a load of homework to do.

The next day, Dennis showed up after dinner had been served. "Where have you been? Lawrence asked, irritated.

"At school!" Dennis snapped, "I have to get my education."

"Oh, yeah," Lawrence said, "I forgot." He gave Dennis a check. "Here, how's that?"

Dennis looked at the check for $4,000 and blew on the signature to make sure the ink was dry. "That will do nicely. I'm sure my grandmother will appreciate this. It's a little late in coming, but better late than never, I always say."

Lawrence said, "I've done everything you told me to; now when can we do the transplant? I'm getting weaker every day. We need to do it *now*, Dennis. *Now!*"

"Oh, I suspect you're stronger than you think you are," Dennis chirped, cheerfully. "I have a couple more projects for you yet."

Anger flashed through Lawrence. "Dennis? Do you know what tactical deceit means?"

"Yes, I do, Larry. And you, of all people don't want to get into any discussion about morality and ethics with me. I could have you disbarred for what you did to us. Fact is, you're not fit to call yourself a lawyer because you are the biggest criminal I know, except maybe your selfish mother. And I'm *glad* I never met *her*."

With that said, Dennis put the check in his pocket and went home.

Chapter 21

A team of doctors from the cancer clinic called Dennis in for a conference. Doctor Davidson and Cynthia sat at the head of the long table.

One elderly doctor, accustomed to giving orders to medical students, made a mistake. "Now, you listen to me, young man. When this meeting is over, I want you to get up there and get prepared to give your father a new lease on life. That's an order; we've wasted enough time."

Dennis let a lot of time go by before he replied. All eyes were glued on him. Finally he began to speak. "With all due respect, Doctors and Aunt Cynthia, these bones are in *my* body, and that marrow is in *my* bones. I will give it up, not when you say so, but whenever I'm pleased. And I am not *pleased* enough to do it today."

"When *will* you do it, Dennis? Give us some kind of time frame. Time is not on our side!"

"When I get damn good and ready," Dennis said, walking out of the conference room and leaving Aunt Cynthia standing in shock—not so much from what he'd said about the bone marrow, as from his use of profanity in front of her colleagues.

"Dennis!" she called as he went out of the wide door. Dennis, you come back here!" His heart was breaking; he didn't like to disobey his Aunt Cynthia. He loved her. She had been so good to him. When he had been in tenth grade, she had taught him to drive her car. Sometimes he would sneak out to Agnew to visit his mother. In periods of lucidity, and in disjointed snatches, she'd told him about her last phone call to their apartment in Brooklyn. His mother never told it all and never in sequence. But she said enough for Dennis to piece the conversation together and renew his vow to someday make Larry pay.

Dennis spent the night with Joey Martinez because he didn't want to face Aunt Cynthia and listen to her try to convince him to "do the right thing."

"Joey!" Dennis called from his pallet on the floor. "Wanna make fifty bucks?"

"Aw, man, don't even ask, what do I have to do?"

"Just answer the phone," Dennis said, "and say what I tell you to say."

Joey couldn't believe his ears. "That's *all* I have to do for *fifty* dollars? Answer the phone? You must be putting me on, man!"

"No, Joey, I'm not putting you on, but you have to say exactly what I tell you to say, you got that, Joey?"

Joey was getting excited. "I got it man. I got it!"

On the third day, when Dennis went to visit his father, he had another man with him.

"Hey, Larry, how are we doing today?"

Lawrence was getting weak, and he'd had a bad day, so he just waved his hand by way of a greeting.

"That's just great!" Dennis said, ignoring his father's weak condition. "I brought somebody with me this time; he's a Notary Public. Name is Ronald Lyons.

"Mr. Lyons, meet my father, Lawrence 'The Arm' Armstead."

Lawrence batted his eyes in acknowledgment of the introduction, while Mr. Lyons took a seat. Dennis was in charge.

"Now, Larry, Mr. Lyons here has a bunch of papers for you to sign. They are called a *living trust*. A living will, if you will." Dennis stopped to laugh at his own play on words.

"Everything is in perfect order. They say when you die, all that you have will go to my mother, your legal wife, Regina Henshaw. But since we all know that my mother is not of sound mind, all that you have, and ever hope to have, will go to your only son, Dennis Henshaw, and that would be me." Dennis tapped himself on the chest and smiled.

Larry was livid. He knew that he was being railroaded. Anger gave him strength. He sat straight up and yelled at Dennis. "What you're doing to me is against the law, boy! You're using your body as a weapon against me. *That's a crime!"*

"So then sue me, Mr. Big-Time Lawyer. Get up out of that bed and go *sue* me," Dennis hollered back at Lawrence. "In the meantime, while you're trying to get up, just go ahead and sign these papers. I'll be back tomorrow to talk about our deal."

"No," Lawrence held out, "I'm sick, but I'm not a fool! Let me call my own lawyer, Melvin Belli, and consult with him first."

"That will be fine," Dennis agreed, "but I'm in the middle of finals, and I don't have time to mess around with you. Call me when you're ready. I may be able to make it back up here by the end of next week."

Giving up, Lawrence signed the thick pile of papers, and Mr. Lyons stamped and notarized each one.

"Now, will you be back tomorrow, Dennis? You promised me you would," Lawrence said weakly.

"Yeah, yeah," Dennis said, impatiently, "just call this number at eight o'clock sharp and tell me what time you want me to be here."

"Okay, then, Dennis. Don't let me down. I can't last much longer."

Joey stayed up all night. He'd been afraid he might oversleep and blow the deal. He needed that fifty bucks.

Dennis, on the other hand, got a good night's sleep, had a leisurely shower, and enjoyed a healthy breakfast. By seven forty-five, he was standing outside of the open door to room 314, where his father lay watching the clock.

From his position in the hall, Dennis could hear very well. At one minute to eight, Lawrence asked the nurse for assistance.

"Nurse, would you dial this number for me? My son is coming this morning to do the bone marrow transplant. I need to call him at eight sharp." Dennis slipped behind the big door and took several deep breaths to relax himself. He wanted to enjoy every word.

Chapter 22

Joey was nervous. He'd had to beat his little sister off the phone at ten to eight. Now he sat with both arms wrapped protectively around the instrument just waiting for eight o'clock. He had plans for that money. There must be no mistakes. When the phone did ring, Joey almost dropped it, but he held on, let it ring five times, just like Dennis told him to. Then he answered, feigning sleep.

"Hal-lo?" he halloed.

"Whooo? No, I don't know no Dennis. Oh, yeah, oh, yeah, I think I know who you mean now. Young colored kid with green eyes, right? Yeah, yeah, well he don't live here no more. You must be kidding, man; this is a rooming house. These kids come and they go—skip out when the rent is due. They don't tell us where they going cause they ain't got two pennies to rub together."

From his hiding place behind the door, Dennis could hear Larry's side of the conversation. Joey was doing well; he could tell by the way Larry answered.

"Now you listen to me. That kid has more than two pennies; he has a fortune, *my fortune*. You find him and tell him to get up here to this hospital, *now!*"

Joey must have hung up. Dennis could hear Larry beating the plastic telephone on the bed rails and trying to scream, "Find him! Find that little bastard! He's got all my money!"

Nurses rushed into the room. Dennis couldn't see them, but the squeak of their shoes and the content of their conversation, gave them away.

"Call Doctor Davidson! Call the ICU! Call for stat blood gases! The patient is going into respiratory failure! Put soft restraints on his arms and legs; he's trying to crawl over the bedrails!"

The doctors came quickly. Dennis didn't recognize two of them, but he knew Doctor Davidson's voice when he heard it.

"This man has a right to be overwrought; just look what his son did to him."

Just look what he did to his son, Dennis whispered to himself. *What goes around comes around.*

They were explaining something to Larry now. From his hiding place behind the door, Dennis gave them his undivided attention.

"Mr. Armstead, I want you to hear me clearly." It sounded like Doctor De Jesus speaking, but Dennis couldn't be sure. "Your lungs are filling; you are not breathing strong enough to keep them clear. We will need to put you in the iron lung. Do you know what that is?"

Larry must have nodded. Behind the door, Dennis nodded too. He'd made it his business to learn all about it, because the old iron lung was part of his plan for *Lawrence The Arm.*

They were speaking again. "The iron lung will breathe for you; you won't have to struggle like you're doing now, but we will need to put you to sleep first. Is that clear?"

Dennis had his fist balled up. "Just tell him you have to put him in a coma, *please!*" he whispered. "*Tell him!*"

But they didn't. Coma was too strong a word to use on a man already frightened half out of his wits.

Just as transportation started to wheel Lawrence out of the room, Dennis stepped into the open doorway.

"Oh, if you came to see your father, you'll have to walk along beside the gurney. We have to get him to ICU," the orderly informed Dennis in a sorrowful tone.

"I can do that," Dennis said. "I'll just talk to him a bit on the way." Dennis took a hold of the side rail near Lawrence's head. He bent over, walking fast to keep up, and started talking in his ear.

"Cheer up, lawyer, ten percent of patients placed in the old iron lung *do* come out. Maybe you'll get lucky," Dennis added.

Lawrence couldn't answer; they had a tube in his throat. But his eyes said if he ever did get out, he was going to get this little pigeon dropper.

When they reached ICU, the nurse wouldn't let Dennis in. "You come back at visiting hours; we'll have him all fixed up then."

"Thank you, Nurse," Dennis said with a somber look. "I have one more thing to say to my father, in private. It will only take a few seconds."

When they were alone, Dennis looked into Lawrence's burning eyes. "Don't look so frightened, Counselor. You'll be seeing your mother soon. I hope it's nice and warm down there."

Lawrence tried to lunge up at Dennis, but he was tied hand and foot.

"Relax," Dennis soothed his father, "I was bound to get you one way or the other. It just so happens bone marrow makes a lot less noise than a .38.

Dennis got onto the elevator. His stomach was hurting from suppressed laughter. He wished he could talk to Alfred Hitchcock; he felt sure he could teach that old boy a thing or two about killing somebody.

When the elevator doors closed, Dennis slapped his thighs with his open palms and let out a hoot. When the doors opened on to the wide lobby, Dennis tried to contain his glee. He put one hand over his mouth, but puffs of merriment escaped between his fingers. Finally, he just gave up, opened his mouth, and laughed out loud as hard as he could.

Dennis was still laughing hard when he walked past the long information desk where two Pink Ladies sat, doing their hospital duties.

"Isn't that Mr. Armstead's son?" one asked.

"Yes, I believe it is," the other one answered. "Wonder what he finds so funny with his father upstairs, dying?"

"God only knows," the other one said. "You never can tell about these teenagers nowadays; he's probably high on something."

Dennis heard their remarks and felt compelled to reply. "Yes, Ma'am, you all got that right. I am high. High on something that can't be bought in the streets. You have no idea how good it can make you feel."

He danced a little jig on the polished floor. "It's called revenge, ladies. *Revenge!*"

His hysterical laughter resounded up and down the quiet lobby.

Speechless and half afraid, they stood watching him laugh. When the automatic doors opened, he stepped outside. They could still hear him laughing, maniacally, until the big glass doors slid closed behind him.

Laughing hard with his eyes squeezed shut, Dennis didn't see the courtesy bus, nor did the driver of the bus see him. The crunch of his bones and the precious marrow they contained could be heard half way to Agnew State Hospital.